I0692200

Spanksgiving

A Collection
of Erotic
Spanking
Stories

Edited by Lori Perkins

For more information contact:
Riverdale Avenue Books
5676 Riverdale Avenue
Riverdale, NY 10471

www.riverdaleavebooks.com

Design by www.formatting4U.com
Cover by Scott Carpenter

Digital ISBN: 978-1-62601-423-7
Print ISBN: 978-1-62601-424-4

"A Super Spanking" by Louisa Bacio was first published by
Ravenous Romance, 2011, reprinted with permission

"Punishment Befitting the Crime" by DL King first appeared
in *She's Gotta Have It: 69 Stories of Sudden Sex*, Rachel
Kramer Bussel editor, Cleis Press 2011, reprinted with
permission

First Edition November 2017

Table of Contens

Introduction

Thanksgiving… the sexiest time of the year, or perhaps not.

I think Thanksgiving needs a marketing do-over. It should be the sexiest time of the year when you consider that we get four full days off from work, too much good food and drink, football, left-overs, time for binge-watching, and the intoxicating rush of shopping for presents, be it in the flesh or online, for others or yourself. And maybe, just maybe, a trip back home to rekindle old flames.

I also love to curl up with a good read on my days off, and I always put aside time to luxuriate with one really good—or fun—book during the holidays. What I love to read more than anything else is smut. I imagined that there had to be others out there like me, so I put out a call to my favorite authors to bring you these tales of giving spanks.

In these pages you'll find some *bona fide* Thanksgiving smut, but this is mostly a collection of hot spanking stories and BDSM fantasies featuring everything from alpha werewolves to strict librarians, and even an installment in Trinity's Blacio's continuing "naughty stepbrother series."

And who knows? Maybe you'll mention this book at the dinner table, and just stop all political conversations cold. Happy Spanksgiving!

Lori Perkins
November 2017

Giving Spanks
By Jack Stratton

It felt like a holiday episode of a TV sitcom, being sent out on Thanksgiving morning by my girlfriend to find a can of cranberry sauce. As I trudged through the leaf-laden streets, I laughed at how ridiculous it was, walking to three different supermarkets in the cold autumn morning air looking through pillaged shelves for a precious treasure.

The big supermarket near the expressway was the only one that had any left. I got three cans, just in case. One jellied, one whole-fruit, and some fancy organic one with orange zest.

My girlfriend Leah and I were having an orphan Thanksgiving for friends who were stuck in the city and couldn't make it back to their families.

I texted her from the checkout line.

"You're lucky, I found some."

"OMG THANK YOU!!" She wrote back immediately

"You are still in big trouble for forgetting it," I replied.

Her only response was the emoji of a little monkey covering its mouth.

We had been dating for two years and living together for six months. It was our first big holiday party together and we were both pretty nervous.

3

As I walked back to our building I did the math in my head. She was just getting ready to put the turkey in the oven and we had hours and hours until guests arrived. We had time for a little fooling around.

The apartment smelled like pumpkin pie, apple cider and spices. I was transported back to being 11 years old sitting at the kids' table, stealing a bite before we all said grace.

Leah was in the kitchen washing her hands. She was in the cute little dress she often wore around the house on cleaning days. A time-softened blue cotton house dress, paired with thick knee-high black socks.

It was one of her most comfortable outfits and one that was the kind of simple, casual sexy that made me glad I asked her to move in with me.

I put the cans away and stood in the doorway to the kitchen with a determined frown, waiting for her to finish washing up.

She dried her hands with a towel and looked over at me, her demeanor changing from attentive chief to shy young lady in seconds. Her hands went behind her back and her eyes were cast down to her feet.

"What did we talk about? Making sure we list everything we need before a big party. Double checking our list a few days before," I asked, trying to keep my voice stern even though she looked adorable.

"Yes, sir," she mumbled.

"I think we are going to have to have a conversation about this," I said and quickly made my way across the room to her.

She jumped as I grabbed her by the arm and pulled her out of the kitchen, into the living room. She whimpered and fought, but begrudgingly followed my lead.

She flashed a mischievous smile as she tried to wrestle out of my grip. It was good to see her slip a little when we played like that. Just making sure we were both totally on the same page. That I wasn't actually mad at her, the sauce was just a fun excuse to spank her, something we both needed that morning. I gave her a wink in response.

The struggle ended at the couch. As I sat down and pulled her onto my lap, she was suddenly still and quiet.

My hand went to her hair. No matter how many times we had been in the same exact situation, her posture could always be improved. I shifted under her and guided her by the hair until she was in the ideal position. Her waist directly over my lap, her chest and arms leaning on the couch cushion next to me, and her knees resting on the other side of me. This pushed her ass high enough for me to get a good angle and made sure that as much of our bodies were touching as possible.

In that position, with my hand in her hair, I was in control of her body, but I was also hyper aware of it. I could feel every move she made, pressing against me or shifting away.

She looked back at me over her shoulder, her hair covering most of her face, but her eyes still visible as she narrowed them at me and pouted. Her attitude only made me smile. I pulled her head back into position by her hair, hard enough that she said "ouch!"

I liked when she said "ouch" like that. The petulance, the brattiness, and under that all, a little note of need.

Her dress was already a mess, all wrinkled and pulled up so that her thighs were exposed. Continuing to hold her hair in one hand I moved my other up her legs, up her thighs, then pushing her dress up farther until it was flipped over her back. She started to squirm again and I tugged on her hair once more. When I pulled down her panties she stopped squirming and tensed. The room was quiet except for her labored breathing.

Her ass was a pretty, round canvas. Her pink panties around her knees and her dress pulled up made everything look dirtier. Her long black socks somehow made her thighs and ass look even more naked and vulnerable. As her back arched, the half peach of her pussy was just barely visible between her thick thighs.

Want flooded my veins, but I held it in check. I let the desire transform into something else, something like cruelty. Then my hand smoothed over her ass, slowly my fingers closing, squeezing her cheek leaving little red trails where my nails dug into her skin.

Then I gave her the first smack. Her body jumped, I felt her against my hardening cock. I slapped her ass again. I was getting the feel of her skin, seeing how she reacted, seeing how much she could take that specific morning, how far I could push her.

The rhythm took over, slow and steady smacks on her ass, each one as close to the last as possible. I could see the side of her face, her eyes closed, her jaw clenched. She wanted to take it for me. She wanted to make me proud.

I mixed up the strokes, letting the spanks get slightly softer and very hard. Then I started building, each strike getting harder with pauses in-between to let her process the feeling. Her skin was red from my hand, her face was red from exertion and desire and shame. It was shame that made me hard.

The smacks echoed through the room. She grunted with each and let out a little shuddering whimper. She rose up with each slap, her knees pressed against the couch cushions so that her ass was even higher.

When I paused again, she took the moment to rest, settling down. I was sure she could feel my cock pressing against her belly.

I took a minute to smooth her skin with my hand. I let go of her hair and rubbed her back.

When I started again it was on the other cheek, the same building. It was a faster cycle though, since her body was primed.

When I got to the hardest strikes she was gritting her teeth and bracing for impact. My hand was throbbing and stinging. My arm was burning from the constant motion. Her ass was crimson with raised marks and a hundred white imprints of my fingers and palm.

When next I paused, my fingers rested on her thigh. I could see her pussy, the lips wet. Her thighs were wet too. As my fingers moved in-between her legs she tensed, readying herself for me to hit her again. I traced the little space between her thigh and her pussy. Her breath caught. My fingers slipped against her lips and she moaned "please?"

"Please what?" I said with a laugh.

She got embarrassed when she was on my lap. She reverted to some smaller version of herself. As I became violent, she became innocent and little.

She whispered the word again and pushed her ass out, whimpering in need.

Then the spanking started again. The warmup was over. My arm went up high in the air and came down fast. Each hit pushing her body down and forward as she cried out.

I knew the vibrations my spanking was creating were going right to her cunt. I saw that even though it hurt, her ass kept pushing farther up, hoping my fingers would show mercy and slip between her legs again.

I steadied myself on the couch with one hand. She had moved and embraced that arm, hiding her face near my hand, eventually sucking on two of my fingers either to pull my concentration away or just to take solace in some kinder physical connection.

The last few hits were so hard I felt like my palm would split. She was wailing with each smack. Finally she turned her body so that she was facing me. She curled into a ball on my lap and I hugged her.

"Shh, that was very good," I whispered and she looked up at me with wet red rimmed eyes.

"I'm a good girl?" she asked in her smallest voice.

"Very good. My good girl," I said, kissing her tears away.

She said nothing, she just sobbed and shook.

I comforted her. I held her. Eventually my hand slipped back to her ass, to feel her fever hot skin. Then my fingers moved between her legs and although she squirmed a little at first, when my fingers finally slipped between her thighs she clutched my arm and let out an animal moan.

"What are we going to do next time?" I asked into her ear.

"Wha- what?" she said, between tears.

"What are we going to do next time so that I don't have to walk around town looking for cranberry sauce on Thanksgiving morning?"

She sniffled and tried to suppress a giggle.

"I'm going to make a thorough list and check it before the day of the party," she said in a shy embarrassed voice.

"That's right. And what do we say after we are punished?" I said, with a little kiss on her cheek.

"Thank you," she whispered.

She was a sweet girl after a kiss. She wanted to be cuddled and cared for. I would happily do that, but I also had other plans. I started taking off her clothes.

In her state, her eyes opened wide when I started pulling off her dress and unsnapping her bra. She went along though, biting her lip in bashfulness.

When she was stripped down to nothing but her knee high socks I led her by the hand to our bed. She sat on the edge looking down.

She didn't know what to do with her hands. When she covered her breasts I slapped her arms away. When she looked up at me in confusion I grabbed her chin and made her look me in the eye.

"Don't hide yourself from me, do you understand?"

She swallowed and nodded.

"You're hands either go behind your back or between your legs, do you understand?"

She didn't.

I knelt on the bed and took her arms and twisted them behind her, placing her hands on her opposite forearms and then grabbing her hair and making her face me.

"Behind your back."

Then I grabbed her arms and moved her hands back in front of her. I roughly slapped her thighs until she spread her legs and then took one of her hands and pushed it between her thighs. She whimpered and tried to move her hand away, but I kept it there.

"Or between your legs. You pick."

Then I stood in front of her and she watched me as I unbuttoned my shirt and took it off. She rubbed herself slowly, watching as I unbuckled my belt. I took off my pants, my shoes, and my socks, until I was in nothing but my boxers.

She wasn't blushing anymore. She was hypnotized by the motion of her own hand. She was wanton.

I went to the bed and sat with my back against the headboard, propping myself up with pillows and then patting my lap for her to come to me.

She turned and crawled to me on the bed, her breasts swaying, her eyes glazed and hungry. When she got to me we kissed. It was a long and slow kiss, with my hand moving up to cup her breasts, squeezing them greedily, possessively. Her curves made me the greedy and the most predatory.

Before I knew it she was wincing and crying out as my fingers squeezed her hard, finding her nipples and roughly pulling and twisting. Her cries were sweet little music notes. The look on her face, pained but ecstatic, eyes half closed, mouth half open.

I grabbed her by the hair and turned her around, opening my legs and sitting her between them, one hand still on her breast, the other moving to her neck.

"Such a useful girl you are with your big tits and your wet cunt," I whispered into her ear.

"Do you like being useful?" I asked, moving my hand from her breast to between her legs.

She kept her back straight for me, pressing against me, hands going behind her into the position I had shown her.

"Yes, sir," she answered.

"Yes, what?"

I slapped her inner thigh hard and she jumped. I took her thick thigh in my hand, pinching hard, taking palmfuls of flesh and hurting her, scratching, pinching, raking with my nails, then up, up to her wet pussy, two fingers slipping into her tightness.

"Yes- I like- being- useful," she said, her words broken by gasps.

"A useful girl for me," I corrected.

"I like being a useful girl for you, sir" she repeated.

Then, with her eyes closed, she whispered, "I like when you use my big tits and my wet pussy."

Then my finger found the hardness of her clit and I rubbing just around it in small circles. She tensed and shook as I followed the rhythm of her rocking hips and continued my little orbit.

"Fuck, that's perfect," she mumbled.

I smiled wide. I smiled because she gave me exactly what I wanted, a reason to spank her more.

I pushed her forward, pulled her onto her knees, forced her face into the mattress.

"What have I said about that kind of language in our home?" I said, smacking her ass hard twice.

"I'm sorry!" she whimpered, the switch between pleasure and abrupt pain making her body writhe.

Here is a little secret: the key is cycles. Adrenaline makes you go up and then you come down, but only for a little while. When you are ready for the next iteration, you can go longer and harder. Arousal also has an amazing effect on pain tolerance. When someone is primed to fuck, they can take far more. Keeping that in mind I hit her hard on the ass, my hand still sore.

On her knees with her head down, her ass and pussy were completely exposed. I moved the spanking down to her thighs, which were far more tender, and then swatted at her pussy, making her squirm to get away.

I moved beside her and put my hand on the back of her neck, holding her down like an animal, and continued to move from hard fast slaps on her ass to lighter slaps on her thighs and pussy, back to hard spanks.

When her moans and whimpers turned into real cries

I moved my red hand back between her legs and pushed two fingers back into her pussy. The sound she made was a lovely choking gasp.

I continued the cycle. Fingering her until she was on the edge, then moving back to spanking her. When she got comfortable with any sensation, I changed it.

When I couldn't take it anymore and needed to fuck her, I laid her out on the bed, face down, and straddled her ass.

"Are you ready to be my little slut? Are you ready to get fucked?"

She looked back , her eyes big, nodding her head furiously.

"Yes, please, yes!"

That was the tough part. It was so nice to tease her, to deny her, to hear her beg, but I just couldn't keep myself from fucking her any longer.

I leaned over to my bedside table and got a condom and a toy. The Hitachi was a prize, because she really was being a very good girl. I put it in her hand and pushed it under her, letting her press it against her clit.

I held her down by the back of her neck, and slapped her ass one more time.

"Be a good girl and keep that on your clit and push your ass up for me," I said listening to the buzzing of the toy and her quickening breath.

She did, giving me a perfect angle. I straddled her legs and slipped the condom on and then slipped my cock into her.

That was it. She pushed her ass into every thrust and she ground against the vibrator, ground against my cock, screaming into the mattress.

It wasn't going to take very long for either of us, but

I rode her hard, her ridiculous wetness letting me go deep and fast.

"Please, can I come?" she begged.

I was able to grab the cord of the Hitachi and pull it away without stopping my thrusting.

"Not yet."

She pounded her fist on the mattress and the pout she gave me when she looked back at me almost made me come.

I felt myself nearing the edge. I slowed, feeling how tight she was deep inside. Slipping against her wet thighs. Slapping her ass again, just to feel her buck against me.

"Ok, you can use the Hitachi again and you can come if you can do it fast," I commanded.

She fumbled for the machine and switched it back on. She moved it in position. Her eyes were closed, her hips up high, taking my thrusts.

"Use my pussy," she whined, her voice breaking out of her little girl voice.

"Please can I come? Can I come now? Please?" she begged.

"Yes," I grunted as I came hard, feeling her clutch around me and shudder under me and listening to her scream and moan.

A few minutes later, after her orgasm was done with her, she curled up next to me in bed.

"Good girl," I said kissing her forehead.

She smiled a wide proud smile and squirmed closer to me, tucking herself into the crook of my shoulder. I pet her hair and kissed her again and again until she drifted off into a little nap.

I got up gently, letting her rest. I crept into the kitchen and checked on the turkey and the little to do list she had written out. We still had four hours before anyone arrived. I would let her have her well deserved little nap. She'd certainly earned it.

I poured myself a cup of coffee and leaned against the counter and sighed deeply. Our first big holiday was going perfectly so far.

Love in the Elevator
(Bonus Scene from *Alpha's Temptation*)
By Renee Rose

Jackson

I haven't seen Kylie since I got to work and my wolf is getting cranky.

Usually, once a wolf has claimed his mate, the itchiness to always be near her eases. Or at least I thought it would. But it hasn't with Kylie. Probably because she's carrying my pup. Or kitten. We'll see. I'd be happy with either.

Because I'm possessive as fuck, I prefer to drive into work with Kylie. I like knowing which superhero T-shirt she's wearing, whether she put on Chuck Taylors or heels. I like prolonging the time we're together before we have to be apart. But I had an early meeting this morning, and with the pregnancy, she needs more rest, so I let her sleep in. Now, I drum my fingers on my desk as my executive team reports on the monthly earnings.

A message box pops up on my screen and my wolf is instantly mollified.

BATGIRL4U: Today is our two month anniversary.

All it takes is seeing her moniker and my cock lengthens.

KING1: Oh yeah? From the day we met?

BATGIRL4U: The day you groped me in the elevator.

KING1: I know how and where I want to celebrate

BATGIRL4U: How?

I hesitate, knowing she's not going to like my answer. I didn't actually grope her in the elevator. She was interviewing with my company and a power outage stranded us in the elevator together. She's claustrophobic and had a panic attack. I wrapped my arms around her to press her sternum and activate her calming reflex. That was before she ran her mouth about me. Before I knew she was the hacker who'd nearly taken down my multi-billion dollar company.

KING1: Nailing you in the elevator

BATGIRL4U: Hell, no

I expected that reply. My lips smirk, the thrill of punishing her already making my hips shift to accommodate my growing cock.

KING1: Do you get to tell me no?

BATGIRL4U: … yes?

KING1: My office, ten minutes.

Returning my focus to my team, I clear my throat, cutting off the CFO, who is going on about quarterly earnings. "All right, let's wrap this meeting up. Send the reports to me via email."

They're used to me. I'm always abrupt, usually an asshole, although having Kylie has softened me. I watch them file out and loosen my tie.

Kylie walks in and my heart stutters. She's wearing the same outfit she wore the day we met. Tight T-shirt with the batgirl symbol in hot pink glitter across her perfect tits under her slender black jacket. Short, fitted skirt, no hose, high heels.

"Lose the jacket," I command.

Her hips sway as she saunters forward. She knows the power she has over me, even though she lets me call the shots. Gaze locked on mine, she slips the jacket off and tosses it over the back of a chair.

I stand and stride to meet her, hunger for her gnawing at me, even though I claimed her last night. And on our lunch hour yesterday. And that morning. Still, it's been 12 hours and my wolf is restless to smell her, taste her, watch her come unglued.

I grasp the hem of her T-shirt and yank it up above her glorious breasts, shove the fabric between her lips. "Hold this," I command and she bites down. I groan when I see my favorite red lace bra, the one she wore the first time I undressed her. I shove the cups down to take in her hardened nipples. She's not showing yet, but her breasts have grown, swelling more each day. I measure their weight in my hands. I want to suck them rosy, but this is punishment, so I force myself to be content with pinching each nipple.

"Bad girl," I murmur in her ear as I circle around behind. I smell the sweet honey of her arousal, sense the tremble in her legs. She loves punishment as much as I love giving it.

I propel her forward until she's up against the full-length windows that give my office a view of the Catalina mountains. The glass is mirrored, so I can see out, but no one can see in. "Hands on the glass, kitten. Spread your legs." I nudge her high heels apart.

She widens her stance as far as her tight skirt allows. I press my body against her back and reach around to cup her breasts. "Are you allowed to tell me no, baby?" I slide a hand down the front of her until my palm meets the skin of her thigh, then I reverse direction and coast up the inside of her thigh, rucking up her skirt as I go. My fingers reach the apex of her thighs and I cup her mons, pressing the heel of my hand against her clit.

"Jackson," she moans, dropping the T-shirt from her teeth. I let it go.

"Are you, baby?"

"N-no," she says hoarsely, head thrown back on my shoulder.

"Who calls the shots, kitten?" I slip my middle finger inside her panties and stroke along her dewy slit. "Hmm?"

"You do." Her inner thighs tense and shiver as I tap-tap-tap my finger over her clit.

I penetrate her, pushing my digit into her moist heat, loving the way her responsive little body convulses at the sensation.

"If I want you in an elevator, I get you in an elevator. Don't I?"

She stiffens slightly. I know this is a challenge for her. It's not that I want to torture her—I love this female more than I ever believed possible. But I want to help her overcome her past trauma. With the right measure of lust and the trust between us, I think I can get her to lose her phobia of elevators. I've already had her in a shower stall and that's a much smaller space.

"Jackson—"

I pull my finger out and slap her pussy. "You will yield, baby. You can do it now or you can do it after your punishment, but I'm going to get my way." I bite her ear. "Now, which is it going to be?"

I'm hoping she chooses after punishment, not only for the pleasure it will bring both of us, but because I think it will be easier to get her to let go in the elevator if she's already drunk with lust.

When she doesn't answer, I spank her pussy again. I use one hand to pull her panties to the side and the other to deliver light slaps on her bare sex, right over her clit.

"Punishment it is."

* * *

Kylie

It's a good thing my palms are flattened against the window, because I need them to hold me up. As Jackson spanks my pussy, lust storms through me like a hurricane, making me sway on my high heels. I'd take them off, but I know Jackson will never allow it. He loves the heels. Often orders me to strip out of everything but the heels.

Jackson would never let me fall, though. He must realize my predicament, because he circles my waist with one strong arm and brings his lips to my ear. "I bought something for you, kitten."

"What is it?"

"Don't move."

He eases his body away from mine and we both groan. I feel the loss every time our bodies separate. From his desk drawer he produces a gadget or device—a bulbous metal... "Is that a butt plug?"

Holy #buttstuff, batman.

I don't know why I'm surprised. It's just that Jackson's dominance comes from being an alpha wolf, not from following the trappings of a BDSM fetish. He smacked my ass the very first time he got me out of my clothes and has never stopped since. Still, I appreciate his investment in keeping things fresh.

19

Even if I'm not so sure how I feel about having a stainless steel plug shoved up my ass.

He uncaps a tube of lubricant and squeezes a dollop onto his finger. "This will help you remember who's in charge when we're in the elevator." He rubs the lube between his thumb and forefinger. His hungry green eyes have changed to pale blue; his wolf is riled up for me.

Damn. He's still on the elevator idea. Not that I thought he'd drop it. Jackson King didn't build SeCure into a multi-billion dollar company by taking no for an answer. But I'm way more into wearing my interview outfit to celebrate our two-month anniversary than re-creating an elevator stall-out.

He walks around behind me and tugs my panties down. My skirt is still rucked up around my waist, legs splayed wide. Pregnancy has done nothing to dampen my ever-present desire to be claimed by my mate at all hours of the day.

Jackson wedges the lubed tip of the plug between my asscheeks and nudges my back entrance. He's punished me with his cock there before and I admit I loved it. There's something so taboo, so wrong in all the right ways. It requires my complete surrender, not that any sex with Jackson doesn't, especially during the full moon. He's always rough, always demanding. He can't help himself, which, in turn, makes me feel powerful. Desirable.

Still, I resist the cool metal intrusion, squeeze my cheeks to prevent its entry. Jackson slips a hand into the front of my panties and twiddles my clit. The rush of pleasure loosens my muscles and I inadvertently relax. He breaches my tight entrance. I mewl and pant, working to drop my resistance. The plug stretches me, fills me. I groan, my pussy dripping.

"That's it, kitten." His hot breath feathers across my ear. "Almost there." The plug seats, but my relief is short-lived. The fullness, the stimulation on my anus have me squirming for satisfaction.

I shift on my feet, pressing my mons into his hand.

He clicks his teeth and removes his fingers, leaves me trembling against the window, waiting.

"I prefer to spank you on the bare." He walks to the end of the wall-length window and unhooks the plastic tilt wand from the blinds. "There's nothing more satisfying than your ass under my hand."

I struggle to think of a snarky comeback, but the buzzing in my clit is too distracting.

"But I'd hate for my secretary to hear. So I'll have to use something quieter." He slaps the tilt wand into his palm.

I eye it doubtfully. It looks mean, even with my newly activated shifter DNA, which makes any pain or marks disappear in a matter of hours, if not minutes. Apparently, my pussy doesn't object, because my arousal drips onto my thighs. Jackson's nostrils flare and I know he smells it.

A low growl rumbles in his throat. "Push that ass out, kitten."

Tingles race over my skin, my breath rises and falls quickly as I hollow my lower back and present my plugged ass to him.

The wand whips through the air and lands across the middle of my buttocks. A line of fire streaks across my flesh and I yelp. "Fuck!" My hands fly to cover my ass and I whirl around to face Jackson.

He smothers my planned protest with a hard kiss, stamping his lips over mine, coaxing his tongue into my mouth. He keeps kissing me until I whimper and soften against him, arms looping around his neck. When, at last, he pulls away, he closes his teeth around my lower lip and pulls it out before he releases it with a pop.

"That fucking **hurt**," I complain.

He cups my ass, rubbing and massaging away the pain. "Ready for the elevator?"

I lift my chin. "No elevator."

The hands on my ass roam lower, slide between my legs and stroke my wet pussy. "This pussy, baby"—he demands another kiss—"This pussy belongs to me. And I need it **in the elevator**." He kisses me again, more gently, lips stroking mine, nibbling lightly. "You know you're safe with me. If you get scared, I'll take care of you. You're mine, baby. I'll always protect you."

A shiver of something much deeper than lust runs through me and tears prick my eyes. I drop my cheek to his chest and press my body against his to recover my breath. He continues his steady torment, stroking my throbbing clit while nudging the buttplug with his arm.

"Okay," I whisper. "Let's go."

Jackson's grin is 100 percent wolf. He puts my clothing back in place and cradles my neck, tipping my head to the side to drag his mouth up the column of my neck in a slow, open-mouthed kiss. "I'll make it good for you, kitten. I promise."

I wrap his tie in my fist and tug his mouth down to mine. "You'd better."

* * *

Jackson

I straighten my tie and usher Kylie out of my office.

"Oh Mr. King?" My secretary, Vanessa, tries to get my attention.

"I'll be back in five," I say. Or 20. Depends on how long it takes to get my beautiful mate off in a tight space.

I haven't officially acknowledged my relationship with Kylie at work, because it's none of their goddamn business, but Kylie pulls the alpha female with Vanessa everytime she tries to overstep, so my secretary must know by now we're an item.

I should probably buy Kylie some kind of diamond ring to mark her in the human fashion as mine. Make sure no human fucks who can't smell my scent on her think she's fair game.

Kylie stiffens as the doors to the elevator swish open, but I place my hand on her lower back and guide her gently forward. As far as I know, she hasn't been in the elevator since the day she interviewed. She always takes the stairs.

I hit the "R" for rooftop. My office is on the top floor, but the elevator goes up one more level, and heading in that direction insures we'll be alone.

"What is R?" she asks. The elevator doors close and her swallow gives away her nerves.

"Rooftop." The elevator ascends. "You're okay, baby." I spin her around and press my body against the back of hers, pushing her up against the wall.

She's breathing quickly, but judging from her scent, it's more fear than arousal.

The elevator stops and the doors slide open, letting the Tucson sunlight stream into the compartment. I push my thumb over the "door open" button and hold it in. "There, baby. The doors are open. You can breathe fresh air. But you're still in the elevator. And I'm still going to nail you against this wall."

Her body melts against mine, breathing slows.

23

"That's it, kitten."

The elevator makes an angry beep to let me know I'm holding the button too long. I ignore it.

"Now, I need you to peel that skirt of yours up to your waist."

She removes her hands from the wall and tugs up the hem of her black skirt.

I use my free hand to yank her panties down in back. My own pants give me a bit more trouble opening one-handed.

Kylie rotates and slithers into a wide-kneed crouch at my feet, reaching to unbutton my trousers. It's quite possibly the hottest thing I've ever seen and I reach for her head, forgetting about the elevator button. The doors snick closed and I lunge to catch the button again, just before the elevator car starts to plunge back down.

Kylie's gold-flecked eyes are on me and her gaze doesn't waver as she releases my cock and licks around the head.

I curse, threading my fingers through her hair, urging her to take me into that sexy mouth of hers. I love when she turns the tables on me. I'm supposed to be the one seducing her, but I see the glory of power and control shining in her eyes, and there's nothing I'd do to change it.

"Fuck, Kylie. Take me deep."

She does. She slides her full lips down the length of my cock, tongue massaging the underside. Then she clamps down and sucks hard as she pulls back.

I shudder, my thighs tightening. I use my fist in her hair to pull her head off. "Up," I command, my voice so deep I hardly recognize it. "I need to be in you, baby." I help her up. Her panties are still up in front, so I say, "Lose the panties."

She does the stripper-perfect squat again to get them off and I nearly gizz all over her face. The minute she stands up, I tug her thigh up to my waist and line the head of my dick up to her slick entrance. One thrust is all it takes to sink into her moist heat.

I pin her back against the wall to get leverage and do my best to dial it back, which results in slow, hard thrusts that send her higher and higher on the wall.

She lifts the other leg up and wraps them both around my waist. I hook my forearm under her ass and pull her hips forward on the perfect angle to go deep.

Her mouth opens in a silent scream, eyes roll back in her head.

"Next time you need to come up to my office," I manage to say through gritted teeth, "you take the elevator." I slam in harder and harder, making her take every solid inch of me. "And you think about this, baby. Think about who fucked you in this elevator." I pump faster, with shorter strokes. "I remember that I'll never let anything bad happen to you again. Understand?"

"Y-yes, sir," she pants, then strangles on a scream.

I claim her mouth, swallowing her cries as her pussy clenches and contracts around my length. The second she squeezes, I come, her muscles milking my cock, wringing me out the way she does every fucking time.

The elevator buzzes again, a loud warning.

Still holding my beautiful mate, I stoop to snag her panties from the elevator floor and step out into the sunlight.

"Marry me." It's not a question, it's a demand.

Kylie's still in another world, her eyes glassy, lips swollen from my kiss. "I already have."

"I want you the human way, too. Mrs. Jackson King.

Ring, marriage certificate, all that."

Her body is soft and relaxed against mine. She rests her head on my shoulder. "Yes," she whispers.

"Yes, what?"

She laughs the husky, throaty sound that drives me wild. "Yes, sir."

To read Jackson and Kylie's full story, check out *Alpha's Temptation.* http://mybook.to/alphas

Publisher's Note: *Alpha's Temptation* is a stand-alone book in the *Bad Boy Alphas* series. HEA guaranteed, no cheating. This book contains a hot, demanding alpha wolf with a penchant for protecting and dominating his female. If such material offends you, do not buy this book.

Tommy Takes Off His Boots
By Ryan Field

After the haircut, Gina didn't waste a minute to ask if her client, Tommy, wanted to go out for a drink that night. She was still standing behind him on the hair covered tiled floor while the beautician in the station next to her plugged in a blow dryer, but the only one who heard her speak was a wide-eyed elderly woman in the next chair.

Gina stared at Tommy in the mirror, and then removed the black plastic cape that covered his lanky body. When he stood to get up from the chair she spoke a little louder. "Hey, are you deaf or something? I'm talking to *you*, do you want to go for a drink tonight or not, Tommy?"

Tommy only shrugged his shoulders and nodded yes, and all she heard was the hollow whine of a blow dryer while he stared at the floor. He'd never been much of a talker and she wasn't shocked in the least.

"Then I'll pick you up at eight?" she said. It sounded more like a direct order than a question as her wrecked, nasal voice rose above the hum of the blow dryer. Her hands rested on her hips and she tapped her right foot. Everyone in town knew that Tommy had lost his drivers license for six months because he'd been stopped for drinking and driving. But that didn't bother Gina Johnson. She liked being in control as much as she loved needy men.

Tommy nodded yes, raised his right arm to wave her off, and loped toward the exit door without glancing back. As he walked out of the salon in his black cowboy boots, he took small, careful steps. He was an athletic young man but he tended to walk slowly on the balls of his feet as if he wanted to avoid looking clumsy. Gina had always loved running her fingers through his thick sandy blond hair. Tommy had that little boy, puppy dog quality she loved in fully-grown men. Oh, the needier the better as far as she was concerned. And now as she stared at the way his wide shoulders slowly tapered down to a slim waist, she pressed her lips together and smiled at how the small of his back arched inward and then gently jutted out to form a nice round ass. It didn't bother her at all that Tommy was only 25, and she, 35.

Gina was one of those women that other women didn't get. Her hair was dyed brassy blond, her nose a little too large, and her chin a little too weak. She had a bulky, solid block of a body that was large, but it wasn't out of shape; just layered with muscle and strength. Her clothes were simple, tailored no frill affairs: jeans, cotton pullover shirts and no bra. If it hadn't been for the fact that she had long red fingernails and always wore very high heels, she could have been mistaken for a butch lesbian, which was ironic because she broke most of the stereotypes about women.

You wouldn't have considered her beauty queen material, but the thing about her that women didn't get was her affect on men. When guys saw Gina walking down the street, they stared at the way her nipples jiggled beneath her cotton shirts. When she walked into a bar, men of all ages, gay or straight, stopped talking and waited to see her next move. It was as if she gave off an invisible scent that said, "Follow me, boys." But more than that, when it came to men she had the unyielding sexual appetite of a gay man.

Gina knew a few things about Tommy, little secrets he wasn't aware she knew. Her girlfriend, Beth, had gone out with Tommy a few times; and Beth told Gina everything that happened in her sex life when she came into the salon to have her roots done every third week of the month. Beth said the first time they went out Tommy didn't even try to kiss her good night. And then the second time they went out if she hadn't been the first one to make a move in the front seat of his truck nothing would have happened. She told Gina it was weird, too; almost creepy, as if he didn't have a sex drive. She said Tommy wasn't much of a kisser. He just stuck his tongue into her mouth and swirled it around in endless circles, as if he didn't know what to do with it. When she tried to get into his pants, he wouldn't let her pull them down below his knees. Evidently, he had this weird thing about exposing his legs in public. He had a nice, big dick though, and he closed his eyes and smiled when she blew him. But after he came, even though Beth had sucked so hard her jaw ached, he zipped up his pants, turned his head toward the window, and started to cry. Not strong heaves and sobs; just a few tears and sniffles. When she asked why he was crying, he wiped his eyes and said, "I don't know."

Well, that's all it took to pique Gina's curiosity about Tommy. Of course she outwardly agreed with Beth that the crying thing was weird, and that the thing about exposing his legs in public didn't make any sense at all, but that's also when she secretly began plotting a way to seduce Tommy herself. One of the reasons she wanted him was because she'd always considered him to be one of the best looking guys in Martha Falls, Maryland. Another reason was because she felt sorry for him. Though she'd smiled when Beth dissed him because while Beth was a paying customer, Gina wasn't the type of woman who would trash a man like that to anyone. What happened behind closed doors, remained behind closed doors, in her opinion (she had a feeling that a lot of men cried after a blow job with Beth). But the most important reason Gina wanted Tommy had to do with the fact that she had a few secrets of her own only a few people knew about. She had an intuitive feeling, a gut instinct, that Tommy would enjoy doing the playful little things she wanted to do to him the minute she took off his pants.

When she pulled up to his house later that night, Tommy was sitting on the front steps with his elbows on his knees waiting for her. He still lived at home with his mother and father, and two middle-aged unmarried twin sisters who rarely left the house. Gina heard Tommy's father shout through the screen door, "No fucking around tonight, Buddy, or I'll kick your ass so hard hell won't have it anymore." Tommy rolled his eyes as he loped toward the car with his hands in his pockets. He was wearing a black T-shirt, a tight pair of low rise jeans, and cowboy boots. He reminded Gina of the way Brad Pitt looked in the movie *Thelma and Louise*. It was actually a good thing he was so quiet and reserved, because he had no idea how attractive he really was.

He opened the door and sat down in the passenger seat of her old, green Saab. Then he looked at the

30

windshield, slammed the door shut, and said, "You look nice." His voice was slow and soft; monotone and without expression. She was wearing faded jeans, black high heels and a feathery white blouse that made her nipples stick out.

"Hey," she said, "Put your seat belt on. I can get a ticket if you aren't wearing one." When Gina shouted, "*Hey*," to anyone, her voice went several octaves higher and she spoke through her nose. Her normal voice was more like someone else's falsetto, or the screeching sound of a slipping fan belt in an old car. To her chagrin, at times, when she shouted or became excited, she had a feeling most people wanted to cover their ears and run in the opposite direction.

But Tommy blinked twice, and then he reached down to buckle his seatbelt so quickly his hands started shaking and he couldn't fasten the belt correctly.

"*Hey*, move your hand," said Gina. She leaned across the center console and yanked the seatbelt buckle from his large hands. Her eyebrows furrowed and she sounded annoyed, but as she clicked the seatbelt so it was secure and tight across his slim waist, the side of her hand quickly brushed against the bulge between his legs and she had to press her lips together to keep from smiling. Then she stared at the puffy bulge and pressed on it with her fingertips. "Hey, what's that in there?" she asked.

"Ah well…," Tommy said. He rubbed his jaw with his right hand; he adjusted his long legs in the seat.

"Calm down, baby," she said, "I'm not going to rape you. I'm just playing around." Then she hit the clutch, shoved the car into first gear, and pulled away from the curb with such a jerk poor Tommy had to grab the handle above his head to keep his balance.

They drove to a small bar at the edge of town, where Gina sometimes worked to pick up some extra cash. When they walked through the front door, a couple of guys playing pool hooted and waved at her; she just lowered her head and smiled innocently. And when they crossed in front of the bar to claim a couple of empty barstools, a guy wearing a gold wedding band and a red baseball cap squeezed her ass a couple of times. Tommy's eyes grew wide and he stepped back. Gina gently smacked the guy's hand and said, "Hey, you be a good boy. I'm with someone tonight." The guy in the baseball cap looked at Tommy and frowned, and then he shrugged his shoulders and lit a cigarette.

The bartender mixed a vodka martini for Gina, very dirty with four olives, and Tommy ordered a beer. He put a 20 dollar bill on the bar, sat back with his legs spread wide, and quietly sipped while Gina entertained almost everyone in the bar. She laughed and joked with Josie, the 60 year-old cocktail waitress, and she told Bucky, a local volunteer fireman, he needed a haircut. When Billy, who worked for the electric company, asked if he could buy her a drink she told him she was with Tommy and they were only having one drink because they had other plans that night. Billy stared at her nipples and whistled back, then he slapped Tommy on the back and said, "Have fun, Buddy."

An hour later Gina rested her palm on Tommy's upper thigh, and said, "Let's go, sweetie. I'm done here." She stood from the barstool and walked quickly toward the exit without saying good-bye to anyone.

Tommy followed her out the door and back to the car. When she unlocked the doors, he asked, "Where are we going?"

She smiled and waved the keys in the air. "Back to my place. And you're going to drive."

"Drive?"

"Yes, *drive*," she said. She tossed him the keys. He missed and had to pick them up from the sidewalk.

"But they revoked my license. I can't drive for another three months," he said.

"Hey, I know every cop in this town," she shouted, "No one's going to bother you as long as you're with me. Besides, you're a big, strong man and you're supposed to be the one who drives." It was true: the cops loved her. And she needed to boost Tommy's ego a little, too.

Tommy straightened his shoulders and smiled for the first time that night when he opened the passenger door and helped her sit down. But when he sat down behind the wheel, he couldn't figure out where to put the key. He searched beneath the steering column, and then all over the dashboard.

Gina shook her head and said, "This is a Saab; it's on the center console, Tommy." She yanked the keys from his hand and started the car herself. "You do know how to drive a stick shift?"

Tommy's eyebrows went up, as if she'd insulted him. "Yes, of course I can drive a stick."

"Then let's roll, baby," she said.

A few minutes later, they pulled up to her place. She rented a one-floor condo, in the middle of an older subdivision that still looked like the 1970's hadn't ended. Her section was stained in burnt orange with chocolate brown trim; the architecture was angular and blunt, as if rectangles, squares and triangles had been built separately and then nailed together to form individual units.

Gina rented on the first floor. When you walked

through her front door, you entered the living room. Beyond that was a kitchen/dining area. And in the back there was one bedroom and a bathroom. She had a second hand, cream-colored sofa and matching loveseat, both dotted with faded wine stains, in the living room. A large flat screen TV hung on one long, windowless wall, with electrical cords trailing down haphazardly to the electrical outlet. She'd only planned to be there a few years at the most and keeping the place sparse suited her needs.

When they walked into the living room that night, Gina said, "Sit down on the sofa and I'll get you a beer." She turned on one small lamp that rested on a square Parsons table next to the sofa.

She watched Tommy cross the room and sit down on the sofa that faced the TV. He sat on the edge of the cushion, leaned forward and folded his hands politely. Then he pressed his lips together, glanced at the empty walls, and reached down to run his palm across the brown shag carpeting as if he couldn't resist touching it.

A moment later, she walked back into the room carrying two bottles of beer. He reached for his beer too quickly and practically knocked it out of her hand. She didn't drop it, but the open bottle had jerked back and forth so violently the beer flew all over her white shirt and down the front of his jeans.

"Hey, look what you've done now!" she shouted. She placed the bottles on the table and looked down at the large wet stain across her chest. "My shirt is soaked, and so are your jeans."

"I'm sorry," he said. He stood up and ran his hand through his hair. "I'll pay for it. I'm clumsy sometimes."

She laughed, then pointed her index finger and squinted. "I ought to spank you for that, Tommy. You're like a bad little boy. Now take off your pants so I can wash them."

"Take off my pants?"

"Yes. Take off your pants and I'll throw them into the washing machine." She was curious; she wanted to know if Tommy really did have a weird thing about exposing his legs in public.

But he opened his jeans, pulled down the zipper, and slowly lowered his pants to his knees without thinking twice. He was wearing pale blue boxer shorts; his long legs were tan and there wasn't much hair. He sat back down on the sofa and started to struggle; it wasn't easy getting a pair of tight jeans over large black cowboy boots. He tugged hard at the hem, to get the back end over the curved heel of his boot.

"Hey," Gina shouted, "Why don't you just take off your boots first?"

"Ah well," he said. He sat there for a moment, with one boot still tangled in the hem of his pants, and then he told her, "I have this thing about my feet. I don't like to expose them in public, is all. I'd rather leave my boots on, if that's okay."

Gina shook her head and frowned. It figured that stupid Beth would exaggerate about his legs when it was really his feet he didn't like to expose. But then she smiled at Tommy and said, "Well then you can leave your boots on as long as you want, baby. Doesn't matter to me. After all, everyone has one or two little quirks... you know, things that bother us."

He lifted his head and almost smiled. "That's right. I mean, it's not like I'm a freak or anything. I just don't like my feet exposed. That and the fact that I tend to hear things sometimes and I can't get them out of my head."

"Hear things?"

"Nothing weird," he said, "Sometimes I'll hear a song, or a catchy jingle, and it will repeat in my head for days."

Gina stared at him. Her shirt was so wet now you could see the outline of her large, brown nipples.

Tommy reached down and yanked off the other pant leg, and then he scooped up his jeans and handed them to her. "I also have this counting thing. Whenever I hear someone count to seven I have this need to salute, a military salute. I don't know why I do it; I just have the urge to do it, is all."

She pressed his jeans to her stomach and said, "That's not so bad, Tommy. I have an aunt who runs into the closet whenever there's an electrical storm, and the glasses in her cabinets are so dirty you can't drink from them. She just puts them back after she uses them. They have fingerprints and smudges all over them. It's disgusting, but she likes them that way. If the glasses are too clean it makes her so crazy she can't sleep at night."

Tommy's brown eyes were brighter than they had been all night. He sat back on the sofa in his blue boxer shorts and spread his legs wide. It occurred to her that confessing a few of his quirks had made him relax a little. "I'll go put these things in the washer and I'll be right back," she said.

When she returned a few minutes later, he sat up straight and clutched the sofa cushion. Gina had removed almost all of her clothes. She stood there smiling, wearing nothing but a tight black thong and black high heels. Her body was large, but it was firm and smooth. There wasn't any sagging or an ounce of cellulite, or a wrinkle anywhere. Her firm breasts scooped down a little and her nipples pointed in opposite directions.

He blinked and asked, "What are you doing?"

"Let's have a little fun. Do you trust me?"

He nodded. "Yes. I trust you."

"Good. Now pay attention to me. I know exactly what I'm doing."

She was holding a red plastic kitchen spatula in her right hand. She spread her legs wide, pointed the spatula at Tommy, and counted to seven. When she said, "seven," he raised his arm and saluted her. Then she smiled and said, "Now you've been a very bad boy and I'm going to have to spank you, Tommy."

"*Spank* me?"

She nodded. "Yes. You've been a naughty boy and you need a spanking. Turn around and bend over."

At first he clenched his fists and gaped at the red spatula. But when he saw that she was smiling, he stood from the sofa and removed the rest of his clothes... All but the boots. Gina cracked the spatula against her thigh and smiled. He had one of those thick, floppy dicks that bounce around when they are semi-erect. It looked juicy; she licked her lips. When he turned around to lean over the back of the sofa, she saw that his ass was round and firm and there wasn't much hair there either. He leaned over so his ass would be higher, and then he arched his back and spread his legs a little wider so she could spank him. He didn't put up an ounce of resistance.

She bit her bottom lip and crossed the room. Then she gently tapped his ass with the spatula, counting out loud with each smack. Each time she reached seven, she tapped harder and Tommy raised his arm to salute. There was something about this saluting quirk she just loved. Her nipples became hard when he saluted her, and she felt a pull between her legs that almost felt as if she were being fucked. She'd been spanking guys since she was 20 years old, but Tommy was different, and she knew he liked being controlled and dominated. It occurred to her that his obsessive quirks only made it more fun. When she began to alternate spanks, with the palm of her hand and the spatula, he leaned all the way over the back of the sofa and stretched his long legs out, inviting her to continue.

She spanked him in regular intervals: seven smacks on the ass, and he always followed with a salute on the seventh smack. His ass started to turn red, but his eyes were rolling and he clutched the back of the sofa so hard his knuckles turned white. The more she spanked, the more he seemed to want.

"Hey, do you know the *Macy's* thing?" she asked. Her voice went even higher and more nasal than usual. She knelt down on the sofa cushions and pressed her tits against his back. She wanted to get into his head, to do something he would remember for a long time. She had a feeling he was a total submissive and that if she did this he wouldn't be able to get it out of his head.

"The *Macy's* thing?" he asked. His voice went lower; he had trouble catching his breath.

"Yeah," she said, "You know, that *Macy's* thing we used to say when we were kids."

"I never did that," he said. "I never heard of it."

"Well I did," she said. "Just pay attention and I'll do it for you. You're going to love this."

Then she rubbed her tits against his back and planted two hard spanks across his ass. "The *Macy's* thing goes like this: *Hey, I won't go to Macy's anymore, more, more. Cause Gina Johnson's at the door, door, door. She'll grab you by the collar; she'll make you scream and holler; I won't go to Macy's anymore, more, more.*" When she said, "anymore, more, more," and "door, door,

door," she spanked him hard on each syllable. She used the palm of her hand for this; she liked the way his firm ass took each spank without jiggling or jerking around.

Tommy lifted his head higher and gasped aloud. "I like that. Do it again... Please; more, more, more..."

"Have you been a bad boy?" she asked.

"Yes... I've been very bad, at *Macy's*," he said. "I'm a bad, bad boy who needs to be spanked."

"Then you can't go to *Macy's* anymore, more, more," she shouted. When she spanked him on the words, more, more, more, this time she cupped her hand and gave him blunt thuds. She was amazed at how the blood rushed to the surface, turned his skin red, and then relaxed so quickly.

"*More*," he begged.

"Hey, take off those cowboy boots," she shouted.

"No. I can't."

She smiled when he refused to remove the boots; she knew he wouldn't do it this soon. So she repeated the *Macy's* thing over and over again, until her high-pitched voice began to waver and her palm started to hurt from slapping against his bare ass. It took over an hour, but she finally stopped chanting the *Macy's* thing and asked, "Are you ready to take off those boots now, like a good boy?"

He sighed. "Yes, I'm ready." Then he stood from the back of the sofa and quickly removed his boots and white socks. When his feet were completely exposed, he fell across the sofa on his stomach and buried his handsome face in the cushions.

"Hey, that's better," Gina said. She looked down at his ass; it was a little red, but there weren't any serious bruises.

Tommy took a deep breath and lifted his head from the sofa cushion. "I never did anything like this before," he said.

"I figured that," she said. She put her hands on her hips and smiled. "Now, you just lay there while I go and put the clothes in the dryer, and when I come back I'll rub some baby powder on that naughty little ass of yours. And if you're a good boy I just might suck your dick to finish you off."

Tommy turned on his side a little. His cock was almost fully erect by then. He reached down, grabbed his dick, and smiled. "What if I'm a bad boy? What if I keep hearing that *Macy's* thing in my head now?" When he pointed his dick in her direction and waved it a few times, he sounded more confident and aware of what he was doing. "Then I'll just tie you to the bed post and give you another good spanking," she said. She remembered the way her friend Beth had described sex with Tommy, and how he had cried after a blow job. Tommy wasn't crying now. The guy was laying naked on her sofa, without his boots or socks, with his dick in his hand and a huge grin on his face. Without even trying too hard, she'd done something right with Tommy that night and she intended to continue. He wasn't perfect, but neither was she. And for the first time in a long time, she felt as if she wanted to get to know him better. Up until that point, she'd been with a lot of men, and she'd spanked a lot of men, but never one who seemed to want... Or need... A good spanking as much as Tommy did.

He sat up a little and glanced up at the ceiling, as if he had trouble looking her in the eye. "Maybe you could tie my hands up. I wouldn't mind that at all."

That's when she knew she had him right where she wanted him. She turned toward the bedroom and waved her hand. As she glided across the room in her black high heels, so she could get her favorite handcuffs and black leather blindfold from the bedroom closet, she said, "Oh, sweetie, I can do much better than *that*. You just wait there and play with that nice big dick. I'll be right back with a few surprises I think you're going to love."

When she returned, she brought the baby powder... For later. She also brought the handcuffs, the blindfold, and one of several black leather cock rings she kept in her toy chest, on hand, just in case she had a date who might be interested in something different. She found Tommy on the sofa where she'd left him, with a full erection and a great big smile. He glanced at the things she was carrying, opened his eyes wider, and grabbed his erection without even realizing it.

As he leaned forward so she could blindfold him, he asked her a question and she told him he couldn't speak anymore unless she addressed him first. If he found that unusual he didn't mention it aloud. He didn't say a word when she ordered him to spread his legs a little wider so she could wrap the cock ring about his junk. She pulled the cock ring tightly and snapped it shut, and then she told him to turn over and put his hands behind his back so she could handcuff him. The only sounds that came out of his mouth at that point were moans and sighs.

When she knew he was ready for another round of spanks, she made him get up and lean over the coffee table. With his hands cuffed behind his back, she started spanking him with her bare hand again, and then she went into the kitchen and returned with her favorite wooden spoon. He moaned so much when she smacked him with the wooden spoon she told him she would gag him if he didn't calm down. Of course he didn't, so she gagged him with her underpants which only seemed to make him moan more.

By the time she noticed more red marks on his firm ass she knew it was time for a break. She didn't want to spank him raw the first time, mainly because she wanted him to return. She hadn't been on a date like this and had so much fun since the first time she spanked her UPS man. Tommy was one of those men who truly understood what a good spanking was about, and he genuinely found it erotic. She could tell by his erection. It never subsided. No matter how hard she spanked him, his dick remained thick and firm with pre-come dripping from the tip.

After she set the wooden spoon down, she brought him off with a quick blow job. He must have been on the edge for a while because it didn't take long. She thought he would just fall back on the sofa and forget all about her, which was what most men usually did. But he surprised her and climbed onto the sofa. He rested back and told her to climb up and sit on his face so he could get her off. He didn't seem to mind being handcuffed in the least, not a complaint or comment. She shrugged and followed his order that time. No one had brought her off *that* way in a long time, and she wound up moaning even louder than him.

After that, she climbed off his face to remove the handcuffs and blindfold and told him to roll over on the sofa on his stomach. He followed her orders as if she'd been training him for years and he never said a word.

He stretched his arms forward and she reached for the baby powder. "Are you okay, Tommy?" she asked. She hoped she hadn't gone too far.

"Oh yeah," he said. "I'm good."

"Are you sure you never did anything like this before?"

"I swear on my life I have never done anything like this before, but I sure do want to do it again."

She sprinkled some powder on his ass and rubbed it gently. "Seriously?"

"Oh yeah."

She hadn't expected him to be this eager. In fact, she'd learned not to expect too much from any man the first time. "You can spend the night if you want."

"I can?"

"Of *course* you can," she said. "I like you. You're a grown man and you can do whatever you want to do. And if anyone says anything about it to you, I'll take care of them." She meant every word.

"I'd like to spend the night. I like you, too."

"Good. That's settled. Now stop talking and I'll take good care of you."

Then she sprinkled more baby powder on his lower back and rubbed it so gently she barely touched his flesh. She had no way of knowing it that night, and it was the last thing she'd ever expected, but Tommy not only spent the night with her he wound up spending the next three nights with her. The only reason he went home at all on the fourth night was to get a few personal things and fresh clothes to bring back to her apartment. Best of all, as long as Gina was around, he never had a problem removing his shoes and socks again.

She had no way of knowing it that night, and it was the last thing she'd ever expected, but Tommy not only spent that night with her he wound up spending the next three nights with her. The only reason he went home at all on the fourth night was to get a few personal things and fresh clothes to bring back to her apartment. Best of all, as long as Gina was around, he never had a problem removing his shoes and socks again.

A Super Spanking
By Louisa Bacio

SAM *wants outta here*

Beneath the flannel covers, Samantha stroked her most tender private parts, imagining her secret lover opening her folds. She could easily picture him gazing at her full breasts, then dipping down below for a taste. As she circled the nub of her pleasure, Sam felt that exquisite tension increase and she moved her fingers even faster, feeling herself reaching the cusp …

He throws her over his lap or maybe leans her over the arm of a couch, raising her bottom high. As he lifts her skirt, a slight draft skims over her anticipating flesh. She knows what's coming, and wants it, but still feels nervous.

"Are you ready for your punishment?"

"Yes, Sir."

Before she says anything else, the first swat strikes her ass. The initial flash of pain fades into a delicious burn with each smack of his palm. She counts silently, wondering how much she can take before she comes …

A huge thud sounded in the hallway outside her bedroom door, and Sam froze. Then the running water of the toilet flushing circulated through the night. It was probably one of her brothers, just home from a hot date. She mumbled to herself, cursing him and hoping he'd remember to rattle the toilet handle so the water would stop running.

Pathetic. Fumbling under the covers, trying to get off. What she really needed was an in-the-flesh boyfriend. Then maybe she'd have a better chance of getting lucky.

She flipped onto her side, trying to get comfortable, trying to stop thinking, and trying to go to sleep. Then the pressure started. Great. First she heard the flush of the toilet, now she had to go. Running her hand along the cold wall, she stumbled to the bathroom. She kept the lights out. The last thing she wanted was for someone else to know she was awake and to hear their drunken exploits. Sure, they could go out until all hours of the night, but her? No way. She was the "baby" of the family.

Drinking that glass of water before bed proved to be a bad idea. She should have known better. It always made her get up to pee in the middle of the night. The cold tiles against her feet only increased her need. She pulled up the oversized T-shirt, yanked down her panties, she plopped down onto the toilet, splashing down into the water.

"Shit. Shit. Shit," she chanted, too loud for 3:00 A.M. Living with four brothers and a father sucked. And, *no one* fucking put down the seat. Sam stood up, grabbed the closest hand towel within reach, wiped the wetness from her butt, put down the seat, and relieved herself. The towel dropped to the floor. Someone else could put it in the hamper, she thought, as she made her way back to bed. It wasn't her problem.

Sheets still warm from her body, Sam scrunched down under the blankets, searching for that sweet spot.

Before falling asleep, a fledgling thought filtered through her mind: "It's time to move out."

* * *

"What do you mean, you want to move out?" her father asked her across the dining room table the next morning. "We've had this conversation before. You're my only daughter and I need you here, at home."

For some reason, whenever Sam thought of her father, she remembered him in his late 40's, with jet dark hair and a healthy tan. These days, pushing 60, he still looked good, albeit a bit more gray, lanky, and tired.

She glanced over her brother Mark for support. The traitor looked up from his bowl of Cheerios and agreed with their father. "He's right, Sammy. We'd miss you too much. There's no reason for you to get your own place," he said, gesturing with a spoon that dripped milk.

"I graduated from college six months ago, Pop," she argued. "I've been with B&B Marketing now for two years, ever since my internship. I'm ready to go."

After living with a house full of men, with only her two oldest brothers married and out of the house, Sam was more than used to hanging out with the guys. Now, at 23, she wanted to carve out a niche for herself: a home, a quiet spot, a place where she didn't have to worry about falling into the toilet in the middle of the night, or wading through the boxers and tightie-whities in the laundry in order to find her panties.

Jake, who at 25 was the closest to Sam in age, and really her favorite brother, finally backed her up. "I'll go apartment hunting with you. You know you're going to need my sense of style in order to find the perfect spot."

Sam's dad shrugged his shoulders, as if he really didn't believe her. True, they'd all had this conversation more than once: right when she graduated from high school and right before finishing college. This time, though, she meant it.

* * *

SAM *makes snappy decisions*

"I'll take it."

Hardwood floors, views of Ocean Avenue, and if she leaned over the balcony railing just right, she could see the ocean, too. Over the past few years, downtown Long Beach had revitalized, and Sam was more than ready to get some of the action.

"Sam," mumbled Jake through his clenched teeth. The look he gave her was the one he used when she was doing something stupid. "People don't decide to move out, go looking for an apartment, and take the first one they see…" Shaking his head, Jake walked into the kitchen, leaving her to talk with Max, the apartment manager.

"I do," she said, turning her attention back to the apartment super, who looked a bit like an undercover hero himself—think dark and lanky like the hunky Christian Bale's sex-infused Bruce Wayne, Batman's alter-ego, or Henry Cavill's Clark Kent.

Mr. Max-the-Super could be her dark knight, she thought. All of her brothers, even Jake, were big and brawny, but Max seemed more compact. As he turned to survey the apartment, she used the time to check out his ass: very fine, indeed. Maybe moving in would have some additional fringe benefits. He could work on her plumbing anytime, she thought—pun fully intended. "So, can I move in this weekend?"

He looked her over, from her head, lingering on her chest, all the way down to her toes. From some guys, it might have come off as creepy. Maybe it was his overall hotness, or their unmentioned mutual attraction, but Sam felt a shiver of anticipation travel the length of her body with the movement of his eyes.

"As long as your paperwork comes back all right," Max said, smiling. "I don't see why not."

From the kitchen, Sam could hear Jake's exasperated sigh. Obviously not caring about who heard his opinions, he went on. "You need to plan," he said. "You need to clean this place," he punctuated with lifting the grill off the stove and gesturing toward enough caked-in grime to give Sam's stomach a lurch. "You need furniture."

"Dad said I could have the futon in the bonus room. It's perfect. Part couch and bed"—she smiled—"until I can buy something of my own."

"You'll need to air that mattress out." Jake rolled his eyes.

"You know me. I see something I like, and I move fast."

* * *

SAM *sets the stage*

Sam logged onto her computer and instant messenger. Before leaving the apartment complex, Max had given her his contact information. As soon as she added him as a friend, he accepted the request, and she noticed his log-in MaxiMum1 online. She thought about sending him a quick message. Just a "Hi, good to meet you." Or something like that. She wondered if he had seen her name pop up on the screen. Seriously. She felt like she was back in high school again. It was good that she was going to be moving out, and getting out.

"Hey there." A message popped up on her screen. It was Max. Guess he was thinking about her after all. "Good to meet U 2day."

Ah, so he wasn't all that concerned about grammar, and writing.

"*Ciao*." She wrote back, delving into a bit of Italian. Maybe it would impress him. "*Come stai*?" (How are you?)

"Even better now."

Those words hung there, waiting for her to respond. Even better now that he was talking to her? Maybe that was it.

"What R U doing?"

Should she tell him the truth? Absolutely nothing, on a Friday night before she was slated to be moving in? She should be packing. But Jake was out at the clubs again, and her dad was on some date. It wasn't all that often she had the house totally to herself, and she actually felt a bit lonely. Maybe it was the thought of moving out and living on her own. Maybe she wasn't ready for it yet.

"You still there?"

"Impatient one, aren't you?" she typed quickly back, and took a sip of her wine. Might as well jump full in.

"Sometimes, when it's something I want."

Samantha felt that same tingle through her body that she got when he'd looked her over, and the feeling pooled between her legs. Was he talking about her? Did he want her?

"Something you want?" she asked, feeling bolder over the computer than she usually did in real life. It wasn't like she was completely inexperienced; it was more like the relationships she'd had in the past, even the sexual one, didn't last long. After a while, it made her wonder what exactly was wrong with her.

"Definitely. And you've got it. So when R U moving in?"

"Tomorrow."

"Any questions 4 me?"

"Yeah, if something goes wrong in my apartment, who can I get to fix it?"

"Not even moved in yet, and thinking about what could go wrong? How about, what could go right?"

That tended to be her, thinking about the negatives rather than the positives. Wonder where she picked up that trait? Her older brothers certainly seemed to have been willing and wanting to mate up and move out as soon as possible. In fact, Sal had married his high-school sweetheart the summer after graduating from high school. While things were rocky every now and then, they seemed to have weathered through the storm of young love easily enough.

She phased out again, thinking about the possibilities of that statement.

"Well, guess you're not interested..."

"I'm here," she typed quickly. "What are you doing tonight?"

"You mean besides waiting for a new tenant to move in tomorrow? Thinking about what might be. Studying for a law exam. How come you're not packing?"

Studying? So he did more than manage the apartments.

"Don't feel like it. Need some incentive."

"I've got plenty of incentive over here. Sounds like someone might need a little spanking in order to get her moving."

Sam felt her cheeks flush—upper and lower. Spanking? She barely knew this guy, yet he'd tapped into her innermost fantasy: being spanked. Losing control. Feeling a firm hand on her bottom. Did she project something?

"Did I shock you?"

"No. Just wondering. How would you do it?"

"Do what?"

"Spank me? Would I have to be a bad girl?"

"Do I need a reason?"

Fingers hovering over the keyboard, Sam thought about her response. Should she remain safe? Stay home until who knows when, or go for it, and potentially get hurt? Hurt not physically, but emotionally?

She thought about one thing they told nervous clients at work: no risk, no potential.

Before she could think it through even more, she responded. "I can be as bad as you want me to be."

"Good. See you tomorrow."

* * *

SAM *gets lucky*

After unlocking the security door, Sam headed up the stairs to her third-floor apartment, slightly hesitating at the second-floor landing where Max, the apartment manager, lived. Would it seem too desperate if she stopped by to let him know she had arrived, and checked him out just one more time? Damn, it had been way too long since she'd gone out on a real date. Sure, she'd been asked out here and there, but not many guys returned for a second date under the scrutiny of her brothers. The few who did often ended up hanging with the "guys" rather

51

than her. And it wasn't like she could ever get lucky living at home.

That instant attraction to Max seemed like more than a casual, "hey, he's hot" thing. She wanted to know more about him, and certainly wanted to see more of him. Maybe this whole moving-out thing was freeing up her mind.

First things first, though. She needed to get her stuff moved into the apartment, and then maybe—afterward— she could spend a bit more time thinking about the possibilities of Max, or dating in general.

Holding the envelope with keys she'd picked up earlier, Sam climbed the final flight and opened the door to *her* apartment. She'd barely crossed the threshold when the buzzer announced visitors. She got an extra kick, pressing the intercom: "Yes, hello?"

"Hey, dollface, it's Tony," another brother said. "We're here with your stuff. Let us in."

Barely able to control her excitement, Sam pressed the pound key, sending down an electronic welcome that would grant access to her movers. That was definitely one good thing about having so many older brothers: plenty of muscle around to help move her stuff.

Minutes later, the first of the furniture arrived. Sal and Tony led the pack, carrying her new dining room table. Sure, at home, it acted as the game table for longer than she could remember, but now it would have more everyday purposes. As Tony raised his eyebrows in question, Sam gestured toward the miniscule square tiled in yellow-flowered linoleum. Who knew moving out would feel so good? It could only get better.

* * *

SAM *wonders when her legs had time to get so hairy*

If she was home, Sam would easily borrow Jake's Skin So Soft shaving cream and grab one of the everlasting disposable razors from the hall closet. She never had to buy them; it wasn't like the supply ever ran out, and a razor was a razor, right?

Six forty P.M. A glance at the clock told her time to glam up was running on empty. Less than 20 minutes and Max would be there. After another steamy, late-night chat session, Max had actually asked her out. The Betsey Johnson sexy baby-doll—her one real girlie dress, thanks to a shopping trip and the insistence of Jake—would not be so sexy with hairy legs. She might not know everything, but she did know that.

Shit. Shit. Shit.

She hit Jake's speed-dial number, and prayed he picked up. It was too early in the evening for his nighttime adventures.

"*Ciao, bella.*" Her brother's voice had the ability to calm her down instantly.

Then: "You did what? Tell me you didn't." After she explained the sitch, he didn't seem too calm himself.

"Come on, Jakie, I need your help."

"All right. You just shocked me. You do know you have to buy your own damn razors, right? The closet doesn't buy them."

The solution was so simple. She should have thought of it, but hadn't: opaque tights. Black ones. Nighttime. Winter. Totally acceptable. Now, only to find them. Since she hadn't finished unpacking yet, she hit the boxes.

She found one labeled: "Bedroom. Sam's Undies," and sent out a mental, "Thank you, Jake" for filling out the labels.

Peeling off the packing tape, she sorted through the lace undergarments, push-up bras, mismatched socks, and there they were: her black tights.

"Make sure they're clean," Jake's advice echoed through her thoughts. She lifted the feet to her nose and inhaled. Good to go. Then she thought about it some more, and lifted the crotch up for a whiff.

Oh, yeah, she'd worn them, but only once, and there was no way Max was getting that close to her coochie.

* * *

SAM *learns a lesson*

"Didn't I suggest to you that you pick up your new apartment?" Max asked upon entering.

Something about his stance alerted Sam. Usually, his demeanor looked more, well, mousy, and weak. Living with her brothers had made her more used to men's men. Men who grumbled while they took out the trash, or wiped the spilled milk off their chin with the sleeve of their shirt. It might be a cliché, but it certainly was true. (Of course, this little mental scenario didn't include Jake.) Max looked like he pressed his jeans, for God's sake. Tonight, though, those jeans pulled taut over more than a few ripples of muscle. He stood with his legs spread apart, resembling a military stance, and his steady jaw looked set with determination. A black leather jacket hung loose, and low to his hips, and was that a black collar-less shirt peeking out from below (yes, she only knew it from Jake)?

Then there were his eyes. In the light, they could normally be described as a light ocean blue, but something tonight made them take on a blue hue mixed with steel gray. They looked as troubled as a storm.

If she only knew how hard it was going to rain down upon her.

"Ah, come on Maxie, lighten up. I didn't have time, and I didn't feel like it." Sam gave him her best smile, and he didn't seem to give. "See, I even dressed up for you ..."

Twirling in a quick circle with her arms outstretched, Sam's dress swirled around her, lifting up and giving Max a quick glimpse of the treasures underneath. When she stopped, she noticed his eyes widen in appreciation, then harden once again.

"It seems like someone needs to learn a little discipline," he said, removing his gloves, then his jacket. "And I feel like doing a little teaching."

Hesitating as he approached her, Sam reflected on their heated exchange of e-mails, and her admission that she was interested in a bit of role playing. She fantasized about giving up control, of being controlled. But was Max man enough to do it?

He reached her. Too quickly. His warm hand slid under her dress and up her thigh, resting on the edge of her ass, making her wish she was wearing something less substantial than tights. "Such a pretty little dress," he said, gently caressing the line where fabric curved over skin. "Too bad it's going to get a bit dirty."

With his other hand, he reached up and curled his fingers into her coarse curls, pulling her closer. His mouth grazed hers, and he didn't kiss her as much as breathe the air from her mouth. They stood there for a few seconds, his one hand on her ass, the other grasping her hair. Then he kissed her. Kissed her with all the passion they'd been feeling since they first met. His lips pressed into hers, and she opened, allowing his tongue to probe into her mouth. Connecting. Swirling. He tasted like the peppermint candy he had been eating, and below the surface a quality all his own. He pulled back, breaking contact.

Just from his simple touch, and one kiss, Sam felt herself grow moist. Man, but what a kiss it was. Yes, she definitely thought he was man enough. But could she let go?

"So do you want to play?" she asked, falling back onto her old *modus operandi* of joking in order to lighten the mood. She knew she did it, and had little control over avoiding it.

"Oh, I want to play," he said, offering a smile that seemed to hide secrets. "And, you, young lady are going to get to work. Now where's that box of cleaning supplies I brought you?"

Pouting, Sam grabbed his hand and led him over toward the kitchen nook. There, pressed against the back counter, and slightly hidden under some additional opened, yet unpacked boxes, sat the products.

He shook his head. "Of course, not even out of the box. Let's start with those Brawny dust cloths. I think the molding around the floor needs a good dusting."

"The what?" Sam was all for putting away some glasses and dishes, items that she could actually use, but molding?

"The carved wooden frames that go around all the walls in your apartment ... that, sweetheart, is molding," he explained. "And once you get that lovely covering of grime off, it'll look even better."

"Oh, please." Sam opened the bag and pulled out one of the blue cloths. It felt kind of sticky in her hands. Walking back to the living room, she kneeled down on the floor and took a swipe at the wood. "Yeeeewww," she said holding the cloth up for Max to see. "That's gross."

"Aren't you going to help?" she asked.

"Not my duty. Tonight it's about supervision." Max positioned himself closer to her. "Now, rather than kneeling down on that disgusting floor, I want you to stand up, bend over, and clean from that position," he directed.

Good idea, she thought, moving into position. Though it felt a bit harder on her lower back, she certainly didn't want to be down there. As she bent over, she felt the hem of her short dress lift up. Ah, she knew what was going on. Max wanted a free show. Fine. She'd give him one.

Smack. A splash of pain flashed across the backs of Sam's thighs. She stood up and caught sight of Max. In his hands was a pair of black leather gloves. "Oooow."

"Did I tell you that you could stop? That you could stand back up?" Max asked. "Back to it. Assume the position."

Smack. The second slap didn't surprise quite so much, but Sam felt the flush of blood rushing to her lower buttocks, and redness spread across her face. *Smack.* This one landed a bit higher, on her right ass cheek, and she was thankful for that extra little layer between her and his glove.

Shifting her weight, Sam sidestepped down the wall and bent down to clean the next section. *Smack.* Max followed along. *Smack.* The left cheek now joined in the burn.

Smack. Smack.

Section by section, Sam and Max moved around the outskirts of the living room, and the kitchen, and finally, they made it to the bedroom. By the time Sam had finished the last wall, her legs shook from the exertion of bending over, and she swore the come from her excitement was seeping through her leggings.

Max's cool hand glanced the underside of her ass, and she shivered. Hands under her skirt, he shimmied her tights down. As he got lower, she lifted her legs and stepped out of the hose. Underneath, she wore hot pink boy shorts. She didn't always wear panties under her hose, but she wanted that extra prettiness tonight. His fingers slid across her curves—such a contrast between the heated flesh and his smooth palms.

"What a hot ass you have," Max said. "Let me help you out of these."

Firm hands gripped her hips and led her to the bed. She put one knee on it in order to climb up, but that wasn't what Max seemed to want. Instead, he leaned her over the side, her butt jutting out once again. Coolness washed over her skin as he lifted her dress.

"Such pretty feminine little panties," he commented. "Who would have guessed that the tomboy wore such colors?"

He'd found her weakness; Sam felt her face flush anew. Outside, she might be as harsh as a guy. But alone, and inside, she desired girlie things. The world was just foreign to her.

"Too bad you're going to have to lose these for what I want to do next."

The briefs easily slid over her hips and legs. She stepped out of one leg, then the other, exposing herself further to him. She nervously wondered how she really had gotten into this situation. Then he slid a finger in her slit and she lost all hesitation.

She shuddered beneath his touch. It had been a long time since a man had touched her in such a way, and never really in-depth. Hell, she rarely had the personal space to be alone with a man.

"So wet. Is this all for me?"

"Yes," she said, her breathing growing heavier.

"Tell me. Tell me."

"I'm wet for you. I want you."

"Not quite yet. I have some other plans first." Max reached one hand under her dress and fingered a nipple. Already hard, it reached new peaks beneath his manipulation. The other hand moved around to her front and found her nub. As the rhythm started, Sam felt her legs weaken, and she leaned back into Max. Into his hardness pressing against her. *Definitely man enough*, Sam thought.

Her ass felt like it was on fire, and she pressed it against Max as he continued to touch her. Already wound tight, she could feel a release coming on quickly. Fingers continuing to move, Max leaned over and sucked lightly on the back of the neck. The added sensation broke through her self-restraint, and she shuddered within her arms.

Ever so slowly, he continued to rub her, stretching out the pleasure until she lay limp. She felt good, but also a little selfish.

"Let me do something for you," she said, reaching over to rub the apparent bulge through Max's even-tighter jeans.

He laid his hand over her roving one, settling it and pressing down even harder. With the skills of his fingers, she could readily imagine the pleasure he could dish out with his cock.

"There's plenty of time for that. You're used to doing for others. Let this be about you." With that, he settled her back on the bed and lifted off her dress, drinking in her naked body with his eyes before tucking her into the covers.

"Next time, you'll owe me one."

* * *

SAM *gets ready to get laid*

Throughout the day, the anticipation built, making it almost impossible to concentrate on work. Every time Sam thought about Max, and their encounter a few nights before, a sizzle would spread through her body, and truth be told, most of the sensation centered in her core. That is, between her legs. She ached to be filled by him. Since tonight she planned to be more naked than dressed, clothes didn't really matter. Did they? Well, look what had happened the previous night. She said the wrong thing, and the next thing she knew, she was bent over, polishing hard wood, and getting smacked on the ass by Sir Max-a-lot. What if wearing the wrong outfit also sent him over the edge? Sam shivered in anticipation. There had to be that perfect blend of the right-wrong outfit. Maybe a shopping trip was in order.

A few blocks from her apartment was the Purple Onion. What a name for a sex shop. She wondered if it was a euphemism for the female anatomy. Maybe something Georgia O'Keefe would paint. Rather than a blossoming flower, it could be a blossoming onion. For men, if an object resembled a penis, it was considered a phallic symbol. What was the terminology for women? Ah, it's a yonic symbol.

Inside the Purple Onion, Sam's plan of attack was to stroll through the aisles and not look too closely at the objects. As soon as she stepped one foot over the threshold, however, a "helpful" store employee was there, offering to demonstrate selections. She stopped in front of the flavored oils section: Marshmallow. Cherry. Key lime pie. Chocolate. So many flavors to choose from. Sam imagined licking a snickerdoodle off Max's Snicker-do-dat, and creamed her pants for the third time in one day. If she didn't get some tonight, she wasn't quite sure what she was going to do. Maybe visit the vibrating members section. She perused the dildos, giggling at that name, let alone by being in a sex shop all by her lonesome, and decided to throw in a little number after all. Who knew when a girl needed to have a little fun, all on her own?

"Don't forget the batteries," the store clerk told her upon checkout. With a bag full of new toys, it felt like Christmas morning, except these toys were definitely not Santa-rated, only for kiddies on the naughty list.

* * *

SAM *turns the tables*

The French maid outfit made Sam feel like she was dressing up for a Halloween sex party. When it came to costumes, though, she usually went for comfortable and easy rather than slutty. After her last encounter with Max, she couldn't help but buy the get-up when she saw it at the sex shop. If it was clean he wanted, then she could be Ms. Clean for him.

In fact, she'd polish his cock so he'd never forget it, she thought, smiling at the fantasy.

Rather than keeping her hair straight as usual, she

decided to do curls. Of course, her fave stylist of choice, Jake, made himself available to her.

She sat on the hamper, listening to Jake banter as he twisted her hair around a spiral rod.

"So last night, Tyler and I decided to hit the newest club in Hollywood," he continued. "Man-Go opened last month and I hadn't yet been."

"Do you mean mango like the fruit?" she interrupted.

"Nope. Man-Go. There's a hyphen in there for emphasis. As if there would be any question. The club has the prettiest go-go dancers in these tight tropical shorts. I swear if I wasn't already gay, it would turn me."

* * *

Max. Maxwell. The name and the look reminded Sam of the tongue-in-cheek secret agent she used to watch on television during the afternoons. She thought there was something slightly sexy about Maxwell Smart, and she always fantasized about being Agent 99. While pretty, 99 also could kick some bad-guy ass.

Right now about the only thing Sam could really think about was getting herself some of that ass. After their previous encounter, even though Mr. Secret Agent Man had left her satisfied, there still were plenty of urges she wished to explore. Moving out on her own was proving to be even better than she'd anticipated.

Maybe she'd purposely spill orange juice across the counter, and let it dry into a clumped mess, just waiting for Max to find it. Sam sighed. Pretty sick to have thoughts of housecleaning and sex mixed together. Pretty soon she'd make herself come while scrubbing the bathtub. She laughed. Maybe she should sneak out one of those toys she'd bought. Give it a little run-through. Mr. Pecker might be a good substitute, but she was more than ready for the real thing.

By the time Max had arrived, Sam felt more than ready for a little bit of playtime. As soon as he entered her apartment, the air felt charged, as if the dynamic attraction between them set off an invisible electric current.

Dressed to hit the town, he looked hotter than ever. Samantha momentarily thought it would be a waste to ruin his plans for the evening, but she had some of her own. Plus, the sexy maid's outfit should have been an immediate tipoff that the agenda had changed.

"I'd like to go under *cover* with you," she said, as she pressed herself against his body.

Picking up on her clues right away, Max responded, "Would you like to play with Mr. Smart?"

And, oh, how did she? After living so long with her brothers, Sam felt like she had lost her feminine self. Sure, some women may embrace the opposite role and "mother" the men in her family, but as the baby of the group, Samantha never fit into that position. Being on her own and with a man like Max who treated her like a real woman brought it all back again.

Max caught her hand in his, pulling it up above her head and pinning her with his weight and gaze. Sam looked into the depths of his eyes and saw her own desire reflected there. His cock pressed against her hip, and then his lips brushed against hers, taking away all errant thought.

She wanted him. Now. And forever. How could she have known him for such a short time and already feel like she couldn't live without him? She'd moved out to

63

escape the men in her life, only to run into the arms of another. Although in all honesty, Max's arms felt pretty damn good.

Twisting away from his kiss, Sam said, "Wait." She drew air in deeply, catching not only her breath, but her senses.

The look on Max's face appeared confused: a mixture of obvious passion and self-restraint.

"What, lovely?" Max asked, trailing his fingertips up her side and inducing shimmers of pleasure that traveled through the rest of her body.

"Why? Why me?" Sam asked, voicing her fears. "Why now?"

His smile disarmed her. "Why not now? When else?" he replied. "I've only met you."

"No, bigger picture. Why did you come into my life now?"

Max leaned back on his side, letting go of her hand and running it instead through his thick hair, leaving parts of it sticking up. *He looks pretty adorable that way*, Sam thought, *a little bit less than perfect.* She'd love to see what he looked like when he first woke up in the morning. In fact, make that every morning.

"What's going on here, Sam?" he asked.

She didn't quite know, and that was part of the problem. Rather than continuing to question why they'd come together, though, she decided to follow the old saying, actions speak louder than words.

Sam pushed Max up against the wall, thinking the turn of affairs was more than fair game. She inhaled his scent deeply. He smelled clean and fresh, almost like a clear day in the mountains, with something definitely wild beneath the surface.

"So what do you have in mind?" he started to ask. She laid her mouth against his, her tongue plunging past his lips and finding the deliciousness of his tongue. She took his tongue into her mouth and gently started sucking on it, giving him a glimpse of the way she could handle his cock. To further seal the deal, she ran her hand along the inside seam of his jeans, tracing her way up higher until she cupped the hardness of him beneath the stretched material.

"It feels like you'll be up for whatever I have in mind," she teased, catching his lower lip between her teeth.

He moaned in response.

Being with Max unleashed a freedom within Sam. He opened up the well of her passion. Touched her girlie side in a way she'd never experienced. Tonight, she was going to complete the act. No more waiting.

"Are you smart enough to know what's good for you, Max?" Sam teased, pressing her body into his, amazed at how all their curves joined perfectly. "Tonight I'm going to fuck you silly. We're going to finish what we started, and then some."

"Oh Samantha, you're going to drive me insane."

Sam stilled at the use of her full name. She liked it on his lips.

"Say that again."

"You're going to drive me absolutely bonkers if I don't get to fuck you soon."

"No, my name."

"Samantha," he breathed into her ear. Each letter sent chills down her spine. He followed with his tongue, twirling a trail from behind her ear, down her neck, into the curve of her cleavage. He ran his hands down her sides, only to cup her ass, pulling her tighter against him. It was all she could do to keep from falling prey to his touch. Tonight, she wanted to be in charge.

She stilled his hands with hers, turning slightly out of his reach.

"Have anything you need cleaning?" she asking, taking him by the hand and leading him to the bedroom.

"I thought we were going out to dinner tonight," Max said, obviously taking in the view of watching her walk.

"Maybe a late-night snack," Sam replied, "but I have some ideas to build up an appetite first, and I could do with a hot appetizer."

She ran her hand appreciatively over his crotch, foregoing any subtlety. She could feel Max grow harder on contact.

The other day, he'd had the upper hand, and she didn't get to see any of his physical beauty. That situation was going to change immediately.

Ever so slowly, she unbuttoned his shirt, fingertips flowing over the chiseled muscles exposed with each inch of flesh. The man may look lean, but underneath lay sculpted perfection. She followed the path of her fingers with her tongue, all the way down his love trail, only stopping at the waistband of his pants.

As she unbuttoned his jeans and pulled them down, his cock poked out from the front opening of his boxers. A glistening of pre-come seeped off the tip.

"Someone's anxious to play," she teased, lightly slapping his erect cock. It just as quickly bounced back up.

She rubbed the natural lubricant over the tip, and Max moaned, automatically shutting his eyes. She rolled her tongue over the silky, soft head of Max's cock, and it jumped at her ministrations. Samantha wrapped her hands around his waist, feeling the muscles of his ass tighten up. She loved being in control of his pleasure right now, knowing that all those sighs were because she made him feel good.

With one hand firmly holding onto his shaft, she increased the movement of her mouth, alternating between sucking and twirling her tongue along his length. Max twined his fingers into her hair, and right before coming, he stilled her.

"Not this time," he said. "I want to be inside you."

She didn't need convincing. She shucked her underwear off but decided to keep the lacy get-up on. She pushed Max back onto the bed, and pulled a condom out of the nightstand (thank goodness for learning to be prepared from those brothers). She tossed it to him, and he deftly caught the package.

Still in control, Sam straddled Max's hips with his anxious cock right at her entrance. "Are you ready for me?" she asked.

Before he could answer, she pushed herself down, feeling herself stretch over his girth. As their bodies met, she held her position, reveling in being filled. Max sat up against the pillows, and she wrapped her legs around his back, her clit rubbing against the soft hair on the base of his cock.

"One more thing," he said, pulling the string closure at her bodice. Her top opened up, freeing her breasts. Max drank in the sight of her, then dipped in to sample her nipples. Then they began to move. The exquisite friction catapulted her desire, and soon they lost themselves in the rhythm.

Shutting her eyes as the tremors of passion began to overtake her, Sam took in all the sensations. The feel of Max's chest rubbing against her. The rubbing of his pelvis grinding against her clit, and his cock filling her pussy. She tightened her vaginal muscles around the shaft of his cock, imagining actually grasping his member with her pulsating walls. He moaned and shuddered in response.

"Keep doing that and it's going to be all over, and fast," he said.

"Come with me," she said. "Come."

He didn't need to be asked again, and as her orgasm flowed through her body, making even her toes stretch out in pleasure. She felt his cock throb inside her, spilling his seed.

She wiped his damp hair off his forehead and kissed his already swollen lips. "What are you trying to do to me?" he asked as he pulled out, removed the condom, and cuddled up behind her. As they fell asleep, she could feel the heft of his dick nestled between the cheeks of her ass.

* * *

SAM *settles into her home*

As Sam walked to the door, she took in the homey nature of her apartment. Red floral covers flowed across the futon, matched with cream and honeysuckle throw pillows. She straightened a glass vase full of purple French tulips on the mail table, and opened the door. Jake stood there with a bottle of champagne, his blond hair a perfect mess and a smile so big, his dimples were working overtime.

"I'll take it that last night went well?" he said as he passed her. "Sis, you look totally fucked."

"And you would know?" she countered. "Have you looked in the mirror lately? You're looking a bit smug yourself."

"Ouch, *touché*," Jake said. "So is this love, forever and ever?"

Sam thought about his question. Honestly, was she really supposed to know yet? Although there was plenty she knew about Max, and he totally knew how to rock her bed, they still had a lot to explore.

"Let me get back to you on that one." She smiled. "But I'm sure having a good time figuring it out."

Jake gave her a thorough once-over, seeming to take in all of her changes, from her cotton candy pink polished toenails to her white sundress and flowing hair. The curls he had painstakingly put in there the night before were now more than disheveled.

"Whatever you're doing," he said, "keep on doing it. Since moving out has done such wonders for your self-esteem, not to mention sex life, I've decided to take the plunge myself. In fact, there's an empty loft on the eleventh floor. Wanna help me move?"

Happy Birthday
By Oleander Plume

"You're telling me you've never had a birthday spanking?"

I stared into my glass of Malbec and pondered. "Well, if I did, I don't remember."

Brent traced my knuckles with an index finger and gave me that sexy smile of his, the one that makes me forget my name. "I'd like to give you one."

"No way." I jerked my hand away so fast, I almost knocked my drink off the table. "I am not into that whole *Fifty Shades* deal."

"Fifty Shades?"

"You know that book about the thing with the handcuffs and stuff. BD-ems."

"Do you mean BDSM?"

I stuffed a forkful of pasta in my mouth so that I wouldn't have to answer. I don't like talking about sex, and I wasn't about to start with a man I had only been dating for two months.

"Kate, I'm sorry if I freaked you out, and I'm not into bondage, so relax."

"Then why did you bring up spankings?"

"Spankings are a totally different thing." Brent cut a chunk off his filet and held it to my lips. "Try this, it's amazing."

I ate from his fork and felt all warm inside, which irritated me since I was trying to be cross with him. I mean, how dare he act all charming after making such a brash statement? The steak was delicious, however, it melted against my tongue like butter. Which reminded me of his lips for some reason and I squirmed in my chair.

"That was yummy," I said. "Here try mine."

"I can't. I'm allergic to gluten, remember?"

"Oh, right, sorry."

I drank another glass of Malbec and felt more relaxed. Too relaxed. The wine snuck up behind me and whispered things in my ear that coerced me to say things I normally wouldn't.

"How would you do it?" I asked.

"Do what?"

I took a generous guzzle of wine before answering. "Spank me."

He leaned in close and spoke in a sexy whisper that made me want to rip my panties off and shred them with my teeth. "I'd take you over my knee, of course."

A heat wave started in my toes and slowly worked up to my nipples, the pair of which turned hard and tingly. I hoped they weren't poking through my blouse.

"Right," I said, "the classic spanking pose." This time the wine tapped me on the shoulder and convinced me that I wanted to hear more. "Over the skirt or under?"

"What do you think?"

I shoveled down more pasta in a vain attempt to soak up the alcohol that was clouding my good judgment, but it didn't work. If anything, the sensuous Alfredo sauce made me hornier. An image of myself bent over Brent's lap while he slapped my naked ass danced through my brain and I wanted it to happen. Immediately. I glanced around the restaurant, hoping to spot a suitable hiding place, but came up short.

"I might be warming up to the idea," I said. "Maybe. Kinda. Sorta."

Brent grinned. "Should we go back to your place?"

My apartment was 40 minutes by cab, Brent's was 30. "No time."

Brent's eyes widened. "Oh, I get it, let me think for a minute." He rubbed his chin and squinted his eyes, which made him look like an adorable schoolboy. "I just thought of a place. We can walk there in about five minutes."

He quickly paid the check. We set out under a full moon and a sky full of stars. The autumn air was brisk, but neither of us felt the chill. Brent pointed right.

"If we turn here and walk two blocks, there's a park."

My high heels clicked too loudly and my stride was more horse-like than graceful, but in my defense, I was in a damn hurry. The park turned out to be an elaborate English garden. Brent led me inside a wire tunnel that was covered in clematis. The vines were brown and spent, but still provided adequate cover from prying eyes. Lo and behold, there was a bench smack dab in the middle.

Brent sat down and patted his lap. "Assume the position, Birthday Girl."

I hoisted up my skirt and leaned over his lap. He yanked down my panties and rubbed my ass. "So round and hot. How old are you again? Twenty?"

"Thirty-six. Hurry, someone might see."

"This is the kind of spanking you only get when you've been very good, Kate, and I think you've earned it."

The first slap took me by surprise. It didn't hurt so much as it tickled, in all the right places. Goose-flesh covered my skin, and my clit sang a little song of joy. Or maybe that was the wine talking. Either way, I liked it.

"More."

"Of course, 35 more," Brent said. "And a pinch to grow an inch."

Another slap, more tickling. I giggled and rubbed against Brent's lap, his gray flannel trousers felt delicious against my bare legs. Before the next strike, his fingers lightly danced over my now dripping cunt. I inhaled sharply.

"OH!"

A quick massage of my clit, followed by another spank. Then another. I couldn't decide which sensation pleased me more, the feel of his fingers burrowing into my pussy, or the slight sting of his palm against my bare bottom. The combination of the two was making me dizzy with pleasure.

"Thirty-four, 35, 36, and a pinch to grow an inch."

I ignored the fact that he skipped all the numbers between six and 34, but I couldn't ignore the fact that instead of pinching my bottom, he was pinching my clit, and it was heaven.

"Please, oh, please."

"I know what you want, darling, and I'm going to take you there."

My cunt felt positively fat with arousal, each fold plump and slick with the remnants of my excitement. His thumb found its way inside while the rest of his fingers strummed against my clit. I shoved the end of my scarf behind my lips in the hopes of stifling my high-pitched keening. Never before had I been so completely aroused,

I blamed it on the riskiness of the situation, and of course, the wine. Not that Brent's nimble fingers were entirely innocent, or the crisp night air as it caressed my naked skin.

"Come for me, darling, right here, right now."

My cunt heard his words and gladly obeyed. I bit down hard on Burberry tweed while my body dissolved into a heady climax that caused my legs to stiffen and quake. When it was over, Brent lightly stroked his hand over my bottom.

"So nice and pink. Happy Birthday, Kate, my wanton sex goddess."

I erupted into a fit of giggles, and then struggled to my feet. Brent helped me smooth my skirt. "That was completely wonderful."

Brent kissed the inside of my wrist. "What would you like to do now, darling?"

"Stand up, please."

I took Brent's place on the bench and patted my lap. He gave me that smile—the one that makes me want to do naughty things.

"Drop your pants and assume the position," I said with authority.

Brent put his hands on his hips. "But it's not my birthday."

"No, but you *have* been good," I said with a smile. "Very, very good."

Spank Me, Mr. Darcy
By Lissa Trevor and Jane Austen

(**Author's note**: This is a chapter from Lissa Trevor's
Spank Me, Mr. Darcy. It is a "tongue in cheek—an
everywhere else" mash-up of Jane Austen's *Pride and
Prejudice*.)

Till Elizabeth entered the drawing-room at Netherfield,
and looked in vain for Mr. Wickham among the cluster of
red coats there assembled, a doubt of his being present
had never occurred to her. It was inconceivable that the
star attraction of her lurid fantasies had chosen not to
appear for his opening night. The certainty of meeting
him had not been checked by any of those recollections
that might not unreasonably have alarmed her. She had
dressed with more than usual care, and prepared in the
highest spirits for the conquest of all that remained
unsubdued of his heart, trusting that it was not more than
might be won in the course of the evening.

But in an instant arose the dreadful suspicion of his
being purposely omitted for Mr. Darcy's pleasure in the
Bingleys' invitation to the officers; and though this was not
exactly the case, the absolute fact of his absence was
pronounced by his friend Denny, to whom Lydia eagerly

applied, and who told them that Wickham had been obliged to go to town on business the day before, and was not yet returned; adding, with a significant smile, "I do not imagine his business would have called him away just now, if he had not wanted to avoid a certain gentleman here."

Elizabeth could relate as she spent time dodging the smoldering looks of Mr. Darcy.

This part of his intelligence, though unheard by Lydia, was caught by Elizabeth, and, as it assured her that Darcy was not less answerable for Wickham's absence than if her first surmise had been just, every feeling of displeasure against the former was so sharpened by immediate disappointment, that she could hardly reply with tolerable civility to the polite inquiries which he directly afterwards approached to make.

Elizabeth watched couples head for the staircases and disappear below the ballroom. She tried not to think of her own time there. Where they watching or participating? She found herself seeking out Mr. Darcy to see if he practiced below or if he was amusing himself above ground.

Attendance, forbearance, patience with Darcy, was injury to Wickham. She was resolved against any sort of conversation with him, and turned away with a degree of ill-humour which she could not wholly surmount even in speaking to Mr. Bingley, whose blind partiality provoked her.

But Elizabeth was not formed for ill-humour; and though every prospect of her own was destroyed for the evening, it could not dwell long on her spirits; and having told all her griefs to Charlotte Lucas, whom she had not seen for a week, she was soon able to make a voluntary transition to the oddities of her cousin, and to point him out to her particular notice. The first two dances, however, brought a return of distress; they were dances of mortification. Mr. Collins, awkward and solemn, apologising instead of attending, and often moving wrong without being aware of it, gave her all the shame and misery which a disagreeable partner for a couple of dances can give. The moment of her release from him was ecstasy.

When she saw Jane and Mr. Bingley walk arm and arm down the ornate staircases, she whipped her head about to see if her parents or sisters noticed. Her parents were not in sight and her sisters too involved with the soldiers to pay anyone else any mind. Elizabeth started to follow, to do what she wasn't sure. But suddenly the air in the ballroom was stifling. However before she could go more than a few feet, she was again caught up in the dancing. Over the man's shoulder, she saw her sister's golden head tip back in laughter at something Mr. Bingley had said.

Elizabeth danced next with an officer, and had the refreshment of talking of Wickham, and of hearing that he was universally liked. When those dances were over, she returned to Charlotte Lucas, and was in conversation with her, when she found herself suddenly addressed by Mr. Darcy who took her so much by surprise in his application for her hand, that, without knowing what she did, she accepted him. He walked away again immediately, and she was left to fret over her own want of presence of mind; Charlotte tried to console her:

"I dare say you will find him very agreeable."

"Heaven forbid! That would be the greatest misfortune of all! To find a man agreeable whom one is determined to hate! Do not wish me such an evil. He's merely looking to tempt me into becoming his submissive."

"And are you? Tempted that is?" Charlotte gave her an arch look when Elizabeth didn't respond.

When the dancing recommenced, however, and Darcy approached to claim her hand, Charlotte could not help cautioning her in a whisper, not to be a simpleton, and allow her fancy for Wickham to make her appear unpleasant in the eyes of a man ten times his consequence.

Elizabeth made no answer, and took her place in the set, amazed at the dignity to which she was arrived in being allowed to stand opposite to Mr. Darcy, and reading in her neighbours' looks, their equal amazement in beholding it. They stood for some time without speaking a word. His eyes were just as compelling outside of the mask as they were when he wore it. The cut of his mouth was firm, his lips sensual. She began to imagine that their silence was to last through the two dances, each lost looking their fill at the other. At first she was resolved not to break it; till suddenly fancying that it would be the greater punishment to her partner to oblige him to talk. After all, it wasn't as if they could speak freely of his odious offer. Elizabeth made some slight observation on the dance. He replied, and was again silent. After a pause of some minutes, she addressed him a second time with:—"It is your turn to say something now, Mr. Darcy. I talked about the dance, and you ought to make some sort of remark on the size of the room, or the number of couples."

He smiled, and assured her that whatever she wished him to say should be said.

Elizabeth could think of quite a few things she'd like to hear him say. Starting with, I was wrong about your virginity. Your lack of fortune doesn't matter to me. I will take you until you are screaming my name. "Ahem," she cleared her throat as she felt herself flush. "Very well.

That reply will do for the present. Perhaps by and by I may observe that private balls are much pleasanter than public ones." She raised an eyebrow at him and was rewarded by seeing a faint smile cross his lips. "But now we may be silent."

"Do you talk by rule, then, while you are... *dancing*?" He said, giving the last word enough innuendo that she was suddenly back in that dungeon room, her arms firmly restrained.

"Sometimes. One must speak a little, you know. It would look odd to be entirely silent for half an hour together; and yet for the advantage of some, conversation ought to be so arranged, as that they may have the trouble of saying as little as possible."

"Are you consulting your own feelings in the present case, or do you imagine that you are gratifying mine?" His hand almost touched hers as they circled around each other, she felt the warmth radiating from him. How very easy it would be to submit to him.

"Both," replied Elizabeth archly; "for I have always seen a great similarity in the turn of our minds. We are each of an unsocial, taciturn disposition, unwilling to speak, unless we expect to say something that will amaze the whole room, and be handed down to posterity with all the eclat of a proverb." Dancing with him and speaking thus was more thrilling than Charlotte's kisses, which had paled to non-existence from the heated caress of his mouth on hers. She licked her lips, almost tasting him.

"This is no very striking resemblance of your own character, I am sure," said he. "How near it may be to mine, I cannot pretend to say. You think it a faithful portrait undoubtedly." His body brushed hers as they passed in the dance. She began to feel that lightheadedness again.

"I must not decide on my own performance." Elizabeth pinched herself to regain focus. Mr. Darcy's eyes narrowed on the reddened flesh.

He made no answer, and they were again silent till they had gone down the dance, when he asked her if she and her sisters did not very often walk to Meryton. She answered in the affirmative, and, unable to resist the temptation, added, "When you met us there the other day, we had just been forming a new acquaintance."

The effect was immediate. A deeper shade of hauteur overspread his features, but he said not a word, and Elizabeth, though blaming herself for her own weakness, could not go on. She stifled a tremble and a part of her expected him to pull at riding quirt from up his sleeve and punish her. She hadn't realized how much she yearned for the sting of the crop until this moment.

At length Darcy spoke, and in a constrained manner said, "Mr. Wickham is blessed with such happy manners as may ensure his making friends—whether he may be equally capable of retaining them, is less certain."

"He has been so unlucky as to lose your friendship," replied Elizabeth with emphasis, "and in a manner which he is likely to suffer from all his life." She stared at him meaningfully. Now was his chance to tell her his side of the story. Her eyes begged him. Say the words.

Darcy made no answer, and seemed desirous of changing the subject. At that moment, Sir William Lucas appeared close to them, meaning to pass through the set to the other side of the room; but on perceiving Mr. Darcy, he stopped with a bow of superior courtesy to compliment him on his dancing and his partner.

"I have been most highly gratified indeed, my dear sir. Such very superior dancing is not often seen. It is evident that you belong to the first circles. Allow me to say, however, that your fair partner does not disgrace you, and that I must hope to have this pleasure often repeated, especially when a certain desirable event, my dear Eliza (glancing at her sister and Bingley who had returned from downstairs) shall take place. What congratulations will then flow in! I appeal to Mr. Darcy:—but let me not interrupt you, sir. You will not thank me for detaining you from the bewitching converse of that young lady, whose bright eyes are also upbraiding me."

The latter part of this address was scarcely heard by Darcy; but Sir William's allusion to his friend seemed to strike him forcibly, and his eyes were directed with a very serious expression towards Bingley and Jane, who were dancing together. A slight sheen of sweat slicked Mr. Bingley's brow and he noticed a reddening bruise at the top of Jane's bodice.

Recovering himself, however, shortly, Mr. Darcy turned to his Elizabeth, and said, "Sir William's interruption has made me forget what we were talking of."

"I do not think we were speaking at all. Sir William could not have interrupted two people in the room who had less to say for themselves. We have tried two or three subjects already without success, and what we are to talk of next I cannot imagine."

"What think you of books?" said he, smiling.

"Books—oh! No. I am sure we never read the same, or not with the same feelings."

"We could speak of feelings," he said.

"Do you have any?"

"I have deep feelings."

"I doubt that," she said, trying to hide the bitterness she felt with a gay laugh.

"I am sorry you think so; but if that be the case, there can at least be no want of subject. We may compare our different opinions."

"No—I cannot talk of books in a ball-room; my head is always full of something else." She looked away from him and then to the stairs leading below.

"The present always occupies you in such scenes— does it?" said he, with a look of challenge. "Are you so sure of the paths you have chosen?"

"Yes, always," she replied, without knowing what she said, for her thoughts had wandered far from the subject, as soon afterwards appeared by her suddenly exclaiming, "I remember hearing you once say, Mr. Darcy, that you hardly ever forgave, that your resentment once created was unappeasable. You are very cautious, I suppose, as to its being created."

"I am," said he, with a firm voice.

"And never allow yourself to be blinded by prejudice?" She implored him, giving him the opening to speak of Mr. Wickham.

"I hope not."

"It is particularly incumbent on those who never change their opinion, to be secure of judging properly at first."

"May I ask to what these questions tend?" he asked, annoyed that she couldn't just put her hand in his and walk downstairs and into her new future. He would see that she was well treated and punished only by hand. He wouldn't even share her in pleasure. Couldn't she see he was breaking all of his rules by giving her the chance to come to him?

"Merely to the illustration of your character," said she, endeavouring to shake off her gravity. "I am trying to make it out."

"And what is your success?"

She shook her head. "I do not get on at all. I hear such different accounts of you as puzzle me exceedingly."

"I can readily believe," answered he gravely, "that reports may vary greatly with respect to me; and I could wish, Miss Bennet, that you were not to sketch my character at the present moment, as there is reason to fear that the performance would reflect no credit on either. You must trust me. If there is not trust, there is no intimacy to be had."

"But if I do not take your likeness now, I may never have another opportunity."

"There are always opportunities. Shall we talk a walk downstairs and explore some of them?"

Elizabeth clamped her mouth shut before her traitorous tongue told him yes, anything as long as he made the world narrow to just the two of them again. When she felt she could speak rationally, she told him what was foremost on his mind. "I cannot find my pleasure without knowing why you have treated Mr. Wickham so ill."

"I would by no means suspend any pleasure of yours," he coldly replied. "I do not explain myself."

She said no more, and they went down the other dance and parted in silence; and on each side dissatisfied, though not to an equal degree, for in Darcy's breast there was a tolerable powerful feeling towards her, which soon procured her pardon, and directed all his anger against another.

They had not long separated, when Miss Bingley came towards her, and with an expression of civil disdain accosted her:

"So, Miss Eliza, I hear you are quite delighted with George Wickham!" Miss Bingley tossed her head in disdain. "Your sister has been talking to me about him, and asking me a thousand questions; and I find that the young man quite forgot to tell you, among his other communication, that he was the son of old Wickham, the late Mr. Darcy's steward. Let me recommend you, however, as a friend, not to give implicit confidence to all his assertions; for as to Mr. Darcy's using him ill, it is perfectly false; for, on the contrary, he has always been remarkably kind to him, though George Wickham has treated Mr. Darcy in a most infamous manner. I do not know the particulars, but I know very well that Mr. Darcy is not in the least to blame, that he cannot bear to hear George Wickham mentioned. I pity you, Miss Eliza, for this discovery of your favorite's guilt; but really, considering his descent, one could not expect much better."

Elizabeth thought she looked rather shrill and high strung tonight. Jane wasn't giving her a second glance because she was looking at Mr. Bingley as if the moon shined out of his eyes. Mr. Darcy, in foul temper, was also not looking to spend time in Miss Bingley's presence.

"Mr. Wickham's guilt and his descent appear by your account to be the same," said Elizabeth angrily; "for I have heard you accuse him of nothing worse than of being the son of Mr. Darcy's steward, and of that, I can assure you, he informed me himself."

"I beg your pardon," replied Miss Bingley, turning away with a sneer. "Excuse my interference—it was kindly meant."

"Insolent girl!" said Elizabeth to herself. "You are

much mistaken if you expect to influence me by such a paltry attack as this. I see nothing in it but your own willful ignorance and the malice of Mr. Darcy." She then sought her eldest sister, who has undertaken to make inquiries on the same subject of Bingley.

Jane met her with a smile of such sweet complacency, a glow of such happy expression, as sufficiently marked how well she was satisfied with the occurrences of the evening. Elizabeth instantly read her feelings, and at that moment solicitude for Wickham, resentment against his enemies, and everything else, gave way before the hope of Jane's being in the fairest way for happiness.

"I want to know," Elizabeth said with a countenance no less smiling than her sister's. "What you have learnt about Mr. Wickham? But perhaps you have been too pleasantly engaged to think of any third person; in which case you may be sure of my pardon."

"No," replied Jane, "I have not forgotten him; but I have nothing satisfactory to tell you. Mr. Bingley does not know the whole of his history, and is quite ignorant of the circumstances which have principally offended Mr. Darcy; but he will vouch for the good conduct, the probity, and honour of his friend, and is perfectly convinced that Mr. Wickham has deserved much less attention from Mr. Darcy than he has received; and I am sorry to say by his account as well as his sister's, Mr. Wickham is by no means a respectable young man. I am afraid he has been very imprudent, and has deserved to lose Mr. Darcy's regard."

"Mr. Bingley does not know Mr. Wickham himself?" Elizabeth pressed.

"No; he never saw him till the other morning at Meryton."

"I have not a doubt of Mr. Bingley's sincerity," said Elizabeth warmly; "but you must excuse my not being convinced by assurances only. Mr. Bingley's defense of his friend was a very able one, I dare say; but since he is unacquainted with several parts of the story, and has learnt the rest from that friend himself, I shall venture to still think of both gentlemen as I did before."

"As you wish, dearest Lizzy." Jane frowned at her. "However, are you sure you are determined to paint Mr. Darcy the villain because he has told you some hard truths about you?"

When Elizabeth bowed her head and stared as if fascinated at her fingernails, Jane then changed the discourse to one more gratifying to each, and on which there could be no difference of sentiment. Elizabeth listened with delight to the happy, though modest hopes which Jane entertained of Mr. Bingley's regard, and said all in her power to heighten her confidence in it.

On their being joined by Mr. Bingley himself, Elizabeth withdrew to Miss Lucas; to whose inquiry after the pleasantness of her last partner she had scarcely replied, before Mr. Collins came up to them, and told her with great exultation that he had just been so fortunate as to make a most important discovery.

"I have found out," said he, "by a singular accident, that there is now in the room a near relation of my patroness. I happened to overhear the gentleman himself mentioning to the young lady who does the honours of the house the names of his cousin Miss de Bourgh, and of her mother Lady Catherine."

"You are not going to introduce yourself to Mr. Darcy!" Elizabeth cried.

"Indeed I am. I shall entreat his pardon for not

having done it earlier. I believe him to be Lady Catherine's nephew. It will be in my power to assure him that her ladyship was quite well yesterday se'nnight."

Elizabeth tried hard to dissuade him from such a scheme, assuring him that Mr. Darcy would consider his addressing him without introduction as an impertinent freedom, rather than a compliment to his aunt.

But Mr. Collins would not hear a word of sense and with a low bow he left her to attack Mr. Darcy, whose reception of his advances she eagerly watched, and whose astonishment at being so addressed was very evident.

Her cousin prefaced his speech with a solemn bow and though she could not hear a word of it, she felt as if hearing it all, and saw in the motion of his lips the words "apology," "Hunsford," "Lady Catherine de Bourgh, and "Master." It vexed her to see him expose himself to such a man.

Mr. Darcy was eyeing him with unrestrained wonder, and when at last Mr. Collins allowed him time to speak, replied with an air of distant civility. Mr. Collins, however, was not discouraged from speaking again, and Mr. Darcy's contempt seemed abundantly increasing with the length of his second speech, and at the end of it he only made him a slight bow, and moved another way.

Elizabeth watched him to see if he would go down below to amuse himself with Inga or another. What would she do if he held out his hand to Miss Bingley and she came running?

"Don't clench your hands into fists," Charlotte said in her ear.

"I'm not," she said hotly, but of course she had been.

Charlotte intercepted Mr. Collins as he returned, beaming from his perceived victory at speaking with his benefactrix's nephew.

"Bless you Charlotte," Elizabeth said under her breath. She didn't think she could bear more of her cousin's pertinence.

As Elizabeth had no longer any interest of her own to pursue, she turned her attention almost entirely on her sister and Mr. Bingley; and the train of agreeable reflections which her observations gave birth to, made her perhaps almost as happy as Jane. She saw her in idea settled in that very house, in all the felicity which a marriage of true affection could bestow; and she felt capable, under such circumstances, of endeavouring even to like Bingley's two sisters.

Her mother's thoughts she plainly saw were bent the same way. She was talking to that Lady Lucas freely, openly, and of nothing else but her expectation that Jane would soon be married to Mr. Bingley.

Elizabeth attempted to quiet her mother and change the subject, but Mrs. Bennet was incapable of fatigue while enumerating the advantages of the match. Bingley was such a charming young man, and so rich, and living but three miles from them, were the first points of self-gratulation; and then it was such a comfort to think how fond the two sisters were of Jane, and to be certain that they must desire the connection as much as she could do.

To Elizabeth's utter mortification, her mother went on and on, saying it was, moreover, such a promising thing for her younger daughters, as Jane's marrying so greatly must throw them in the way of other rich men.

Elizabeth looked down the table at Kitty and Lydia who were behaving as if they wanted a turn in the dungeons themselves. Surely their father could do something about that, but he was nowhere to be seen.

At long last Mrs. Bennet concluded with many good

wishes that Lady Lucas might soon be equally fortunate, though evidently and triumphantly believing there was no chance of it.

In vain did Elizabeth endeavour to check the rapidity of her mother's words, or persuade her to describe her felicity in a less audible whisper.

Nothing that she could say, however, had any influence. Her mother would talk of her views in the same intelligible tone. Elizabeth blushed and blushed again with shame and vexation. She could not help frequently glancing her eye at Mr. Darcy, though every glance convinced her of what she dreaded; for though he was not always looking at her mother, she was convinced that his attention was invariably fixed by her.

The expression of his face changed gradually from indignant contempt to a composed and steady gravity.

She wanted to explain to him that it was just the way her mother was and she was harmless in her own way, but the words stuck in her throat.

At length, however, Mrs. Bennet had no more to say And Elizabeth began to revive. But not long was the interval of tranquility; for, when supper was over, singing was talked of, and she had the mortification of seeing Mary, after very little entreaty, preparing to oblige the company.

By many significant looks and silent entreaties, did she endeavor to prevent such a proof of complaisance, but in vain; Mary would not understand them; such an opportunity of exhibiting was delightful to her, and she began her song. Mary's powers were by no means fitted for such a display; her voice was weak, and her manner affected.

Elizabeth was in agonies. She looked at Jane, to see how she bore it; but Jane was very composedly talking to

Bingley. She looked at his two sisters, and saw them making signs of derision at each other, and at Darcy, who continued, however, imperturbably grave. She looked at her father to entreat his interference, lest Mary should be singing all night. He took the hint, and when Mary had finished her second song, said aloud, "That will do extremely well, child. You have delighted us long enough. Let the other young ladies have time to exhibit."

Mary, though pretending not to hear, was somewhat disconcerted; and Elizabeth, sorry for her, and sorry for her father's speech, was afraid her anxiety had done no good.

To Elizabeth it appeared that, had her family made an agreement to expose themselves as much as they could during the evening, it would have been impossible for them to play their parts with more spirit or finer success; and happy did she think it for Bingley and her sister that some of the exhibition had escaped his notice, and that his feelings were not of a sort to be much distressed by the folly which he must have witnessed. That his two sisters and Mr. Darcy, however, should have such an opportunity of ridiculing her relations, was bad enough, and she could not determine whether the silent contempt of the gentleman, or the insolent smiles of the ladies, were more intolerable.

At the end of her rope, Elizabeth realized that nothing would paint her family in a better light. She might as well please herself. She moved to the staircase, dodging soldiers and nodding at other guests. A hand on her arm stopped her just as she was to place a foot on the stairs. Mr. Darcy's fingers gripped her elbow that she was sure to be bruised the next morning.

"There is nothing down there for you."

"I beg to differ, sir."

"Master," he whispered. "And does this mean you are mine?"

She shook her head. "I am beyond mortification and this night is surely the worst of my life. I seek redemption of it."

Mr. Darcy cocked his head at her. "Come to the library with me," he said.

"I told you I do not wish to discuss books with you."

"And perhaps I was not clear that no man but I will touch you."

Elizabeth's breath caught in her throat. "Will you touch me?"

He cocked an eyebrow at her.

"Master," she whispered.

"Walk," he ordered and together they sauntered into the library. He all but shoved her inside and bolted the door closed.

"I will be ruined, if we were seen."

"No one pays attention to such things at Netherfield," he told her.

"I dislike you," she said.

"Good," he said indifferently. "I have a urge to make you like me less."

"I don't know how that is possible... Oh!" She gave a little scream as he crossed the room with the quickness of a panther. With a cruel twist of her arm, he propelled her to the reading couch and laid her across his lap.

"What are you doing?" she asked, trying to get up as he pulled her skirts over her head.

"Such virtue," he mocked, "Wearing undergarments to Netherfield." He yanked them off, ripping them. "You will leave without them."

"You're a beast," she raged, even as pleasure pooled deep in her belly.

"So lovely," Mr. Darcy said in a shaking voice. "How you drive me to madness. Just when I think I cannot loathe your family more, the sound of your voice wipes them all from my mind." He slapped his big hand on the sweet white curve of her buttocks.

"Oh," she hiccupped into the red velvet of the couch.

"This," he spanked her again. "Is for your intolerable manners as we danced." Whack. "This is for mentioning that reprobate Wickham." Whack."

"Please," Elizabeth sobbed. Her posterior was burning and she was growing wet between her legs.

Whack. "Please what?"

"Please, Master, no more."

Whack. "Don't top from the bottom."

"What?" she asked.

Whack. "That is for your mother."

"Please Master, another."

"Indeed." He gave her three rapid smacks.

"Thank you, Master," she whispered. Her bottom was hot and raw from his ministrations, but she felt the shame her family caused drifting away.

Whack.

She flinched.

"That was for your sister's abysmal piano playing."

Elizabeth stifled a giggle even as tears rolled down her cheek. "Master, please." *Love me* came unbidden to her lips and she swallowed it before it erupted into the room.

Whack.

"That was for your idiot cousin who dared speak to me so familiarly."

Whack, Whack

"That was for your two youngest sisters whose behavior is this side of appalling."

"Thank you, Master," she said.

He rubbed his hand over her burning flesh. She felt his hardness pressing against his belly.

Whack. That was the hardest of all and she shrieked in pain.

"That was for making me think of nothing else but your sweet body. Are you going to let me have you?"

"No, Master," she said, bracing for the next slap. But he merely rubbed her bottom, soothing her while inflaming her senses.

"Your mouth says no," he said and rolled her off him so she landed artlessly on the floor. Her skirts were still up around her waist. "But your body begs for me."

He lay between her thighs, touching his mouth to her sensitive folds. Elizabeth writhed, wishing she could think of Charlotte or the damnable Mr. Wickham—even Miss Bingley, but there was no one but Mr. Darcy. He licked every inch of her core, paying attention to the swollen, sensitive bud that had her bucking her hips into his face as he serviced her with his tongue and fingers.

"Darcy," she moaned, shattering into a thousand pieces. "Why can't I hate you?"

"Everyday could be like this," he said. "You are the only one stopping this."

"I...," she said helplessly.

"No more words," he unbuttoned his pants and guided her head to him.

Elizabeth lunged for him, almost knocking them off balance.

"Yes," he hissed out as she took out her aggression by sucking him down her throat.

She wanted to break his calm, his control.

His fingers twisted in her hair, tangling each curl through his hands. She opened her eyes to look up at him and found him staring at her, mesmerized.

"You please me, sweet Elizabeth," he said, sounding hollow and shocked.

Elizabeth slid her mouth up and down, reveling in the feel of him in her throat. Her tongue lapped circles around him.

"I would have you naked, covered in oil."

She bobbed her head faster, loving the sound of his harsh breathing.

"Your feet tied over your head."

Her mouth was making wet, sucking sounds.

"I would penetrate you until you remember no other touch by mine," he gritted out. His body tensed. Elizabeth flung her arms around his hips, keeping him locked down her throat as he came.

"Oh sweet Elizabeth. Mine. Only mine," he roared.

Pulling her head back, he kissed her, deep, devouring. She felt as if she was drowning.

"You must leave, or surrender to me," he said.

"I cannot," she cried. "Wretched creature that I am. Wretched creature that you are."

He helped her to her feet and held her until she gained back her balance. Smoothing her skirts over her still stinging backside, he kissed her and she could still taste herself on his lips.

"Think on my offer. Your family does you no favors."

She straightened away from him. "I love my family. And I am more than the sum of their personalities."

He watched her leave the library with a thoughtful frown.

The rest of the evening brought Elizabeth little amusement She was at least free from the offense of Mr. Darcy's further notice; though often standing within a very short distance of her, quite disengaged, he never came near enough to speak.

The Longbourn party were the last of all the company to depart, and, by a manoeuvre of Mrs. Bennet, had to wait for their carriage a quarter of an hour after everybody else was gone, which gave them time to see how heartily they were wished away by some of the family.

Darcy said nothing at all. Mr. Bennet, in equal silence, was enjoying the scene. Mr. Bingley and Jane were standing together, a little detached from the rest, and talked only to each other.

Spanked By Her Stepbrother
By Trinity Blacio

Chapter One

"I can't believe you're leaving New York to go home. What happened to never going back to Nebraska? Hell, for that matter what happened to never speaking to your mom?" her best friend Taz said, as she sat on the bed watching her pack her suitcase.

"Taz, I told you, I'm going for a week. It's not like I'm going to be gone forever. Plus, you have dinner with Max's family and then you guys are going skiing so you won't even miss me. I'll be back in plenty of time for our next shoot." She shut the suitcase, zipping it up. "Plus, thanksgiving is about giving thanks, so I figured I'd give her one more shot, my thanks for some of the good times as a child. But this is the last shot." Laney sat down beside her friend. They had been friends ever since that first day she had gotten off the bus, when some creep had tried to pick her up. Yes, her friend had not only saved her life, but they had become inseparable since that day, until now.

"Look you are like a sister to me. I wouldn't even be here if it wasn't for you, not to mention a bank account where I can soon retire, thanks to your need to learn the stock markets." Laney nudged Taz with her shoulder. "So, are you ready for Max to pop the question?" she asked.

"No, I'm scared half out of my mind. What if his parents find out what happened to me?" Taz got up, rubbing the scar on her arm.

"Max already knows, and honey you were 17 years old. Now quit worrying and take me to the airport. I can't wait to meet this man mom married. I have to admit if it wasn't him getting growly on the phone, I would have told her to get lost." Laney laughed, picking up her suitcase and rolling it towards the living room.

"Wait, what are you talking about?" Taz asked, following behind her.

"It was the strangest thing. I mean I thought about it and I just was going to say no, but when my mom started to whine, my stepfather took the phone from her and growled. He said, 'family should be together' and that he expected me there and do you believe it I gave in? I swear to God, Taz his growl was the sexist thing I've ever heard." Laney stopped. "Oh my God, what if I'm attracted to her man, to my stepdad?"

Taz laughed. "Please. So, the man had a sexy growl. He could be uglier than sin too. But you are so righteous that there is no way your mother has anything to worry about." Her friend smacked her arm. "Quiet being a worry wart."

"Look who's talking," Laney laughed as they piled into her car heading towards the airport, with butterflies in her stomach. She didn't know why, but Laney had this strange feeling her life was going to change, but she wasn't sure it be for the better.

* * *

Kelton stood on his porch looking out at his ranch, Bass, his second-in-command next to him. "I'll be gone only a few days, but we have that shipment coming in. I want you to make sure that they are put in the west pasture after they are looked over and branded. Also, keep a look out on the west side. Twice now our fences have gone down and it wasn't done by animals." He looked to Bass. "Make sure the pack house is open for those that need it. I have three women coming in to set up to feed the needy, including your mate," he said.

Bass grunted. "Sixteen turkeys, ten hams, and they even have seven buffalo roasts. Believe me they have enough food planned for the whole city. We'll be fine. You go enjoy your time with your old man. I'm happy he's found someone. After your mother was killed, I was worried."

"You aren't the only one. My sister and brothers were too. It will be interesting to meet her especially since she is human. Dad has told her everything and she wants to change, but not until she settles with her daughter. It seems they are estranged. That's one of the reasons Dad has called us all in." Kelton laughed. "We haven't been together for over three years. The house is going to be filled with my nephews and nieces. Yes, it's going to be wild, especially if his lady is all uptight like my father has described."

"You might also be getting the wrong view of her though. Remember there are two sides to everything. Is she an only child?" They both turned and headed towards his waiting car.

"One girl and one boy. Both have agreed to come

and neither have seen the other in over eight years. He left before the girl did, from what Dad told me. Yes, this is going to be a wild week. Another reason why I decided to go in a little early to help get everyone settled."

Kelton laughed as his dog Duke jumped into the car as soon as he opened the door. "Sorry bud, but you're not coming this time. Come on out," he ordered. The dog whined, but jumped out sitting next to the door.

"You be good for Bass here and I'll bring you home a treat," he said pet his 120 pound Irish wolfhound.

"Not to worry, the kids will keep him busy," Bass said as he got into the car, his suitcase already in the trunk. "And for Pete's sakes, relax for a change. Who knows, maybe you'll even find your mate," Bass said shaking his hand. Kelton headed towards the airport, his private jet waiting for him.

Chapter Two

Laney stared at the home, checking the address again. It would seem her mother had latched on to a rich one. She only hoped her mother hadn't attached herself to a nut case like the last time she was home. Taking a deep breath, she got of the cab, paying the driver before grabbing her suitcase.

The front door opened and her mother stepped outside with a man next to her. "Laney?" her mother asked unsure.

Her mother looked the same, except a few years older. Her mother had actually put on some weight and wasn't the toothpick she had left when she was a teenager. "Hi mom," she said coming up the stair and hugging her. "You look good," Laney said, stepping back.

"Thank you for coming. I know we have a lot to work through." Her mom laughed. "I'm being rude. Laney this is my husband, Omar Mason. Omar, my baby girl, Laney," her mother introduced them. Laney held out her hand, but Omar wouldn't have any of it and just pulled her into a bear hug. He was huge, with dark salt and pepper hair pulled back in what she imagined was a ponytail.

"Welcome, we are very pleased you are here. Be warned, my family is also coming so we are going to be running around chasing little ones soon, but you're the first one here. So, let us show you to your room."

As they walked towards the front door, Omar said, "My wife has every picture of you in all the magazines," Omar said. "She is very proud of her daughter."

"Did you sell the old place?" Laney asked as she stepped into the hallway, whistling. "Wow, amazing." Laney said, staring at massive staircase.

"That house was a death trap. We had it bull-dozed down and sold the property. Your mother didn't need it." Omar told her, leading them up the staircase.

"It might have needed some work, but it was built by my father," Laney said not too happy with Omar's remark. She looked up at Omar who was smiling.

"I'm sure it was something back then, but after years of not being kept up, I'm afraid it was ready to fall apart," he said, turning the corner.

"And whose fault would that be, mine, a 16-year-old that was working full time just to put food in our kitchen? Who was also trying to finish school early so she could go to college, with a college fund that should have been there for me to use?" She snapped, getting a little more pissed.

"Watch it young lady. I won't have you disrespecting your mother in her own home," Omar said, opening the door to a large bedroom.

Laney didn't even step through the door, turning around and pulling out her phone calling a cab. "Have a great Thanksgiving Mom. Hope you and your new man are happy. My Christmas gift to you is a clean slate," she said going down the stairs, but she ran smack into what had to be Omar's son, her stepbrother, who looked like the spitting image of his dad, but with long dark hair.

"Problem's already Dad?" he said looking behind her.

"Excuse me," Laney tried to move around the gorgeous man, her anger still in the forefront.

"I'm afraid I might have said a few things that haven't been cleared up yet," Omar said behind her as he reached down and grabbed her suitcase out of her hand. "We don't run from our problems, young lady. We work them out," he said.

Laney spun around, growling. "But you are not my family. I haven't been a part of her life since I was ten years old when she tried to sell me!"

Her mother gasped up on the stairs, tears rolled down her cheeks shaking her head. "I would never," she said.

"Really," Laney didn't care now, she was furious. She stripped out of her coat and shirt. "Do you think I like having a scar run up my stomach? Why do you think I only do photo shoots where I can cover this?" Laney was shaking because she was so pissed.

"I don't remember," her mom said as Omar wrapped his arms around her and stared down at her.

"Get dressed. This is not the place to go over this. You just got here. It's obvious your mother does not remember what happened. This is normal with someone with all…"

Laney held up her hand, snorting. "Let me guess she told you she had some kind of illness that makes her forget."

Laney glanced behind her at the stepbrother. "You might want to watch your father's bank account. Cokeheads have a habit of draining everyone." She grabbed her shirt and coat, needing to walk. "I'm going for a walk."

"Go with her, Kelton. It's obvious she is in no condition to be by herself while I have a talk with my wife," Omar lifted her mother up and carried her off as Laney stepped outside, zipping up her coat, taking a deep breath.

"I don't need a babysitter. Go find your room. I'll be fine. I'm not going anywhere right now," Laney said, stepping off the stairs.

"I will walk with you. My name is Kelton. I'm the oldest of my brothers and sisters." Kelton said, matching her steps to his.

She stopped and turned to Kelton. "Look Kelton, thank you for the company, but really, I need to be alone," Laney said.

The man leaned down nose to nose to her. "No, don't ask again." He put his finger on her lips before she could snap at him. "Be careful, wild fire, because I spank and I'd hate to do that on our first outing."

"What?" she squeaked.

* * *

Kelton hid his smile, watching the little spitfire sputter, her face turning a flushed color. Oh, she was a beauty and one he would explore more. But first she needed to calm down so his father could get down to whatever the truth was, but her scent told him she was telling the truth. The hurt and pain radiating off her had his wolf pacing.

His wolf had never been so excited about any female. Yes, this female was going to get more attention than she had hoped.

"You heard me. Now come, I know for a fact that there is a pretty spot I can show you. It was one of the reasons dad bought this place when mom died." Kelton wrapped his arm around her full-figured waist and guided her down the path.

"Sorry about your mother," she finally said.

"Thank you, it was a surprise to us all. Tell me what happened after your father died," Kelton said.

She stiffened. "Let's just say it's the same as most kids whose parents turn to drugs. Mom got hooked on the sedative they gave her when my father died. She really did love him, needed him, but when he died it was like she shut down. Anyway, the doctor prescribed pills, then the doctor takes the pills away, and mom goes to street drugs. My brother left first, but he was older and had a job lined up." A single tear rolled down her cheek. "He packed up and left without a word. I was stuck with my mother. I tried to stick it out to finish school, but the last straw was when I was 16 and her dealer showed up standing at the foot of my bed," Laney said, looking around.

"It is beautiful out here. Anyway, I got away from him, packed a bag and was on the first bus to New York, hoping to find my uncle, but I'm afraid the street hustlers cornered me when I first arrived. If it wasn't for my best friend, well I wouldn't be here. That's my story. Now you. Tell me about yourself, since it seems we are family," she said looking him over and almost falling on her ass, in the shoes she was wearing.

Stopping, Kelton bent down, taking her left foot and breaking the heel off the boot, as she screamed. "What the hell are you doing? Do you know how much I paid for those?" she glared at him, as he finally got hold of her other boot and did the same.

"Now you won't fall and break your neck," he told

her and started to continue to walk when he noticed her turning around, heading back to where they had come from. Taking a deep breath, he took off in a jog to get caught up with her. "Where are you going?"

"Home. You and your father are totally out of your minds." She stopped for a minute. "Maybe that's what my mom needs—a wacko to keep her sane. Who the hell knows? As for the boots, I'll just charge this up for the last visit with my mom." She growled and stared walking towards the house again, but he caught her around the waist and brought his hand down on her ass hard.

"First, I'm not a nut job and either is my father. Second," he spanked her again. "You cuss again and I'll spank your bare butt. Third, I didn't want you breaking your fool neck. If the boots mean so much to you, I'll buy you another pair." He held on to her, frowning down at her shocked expression.

"You..." She stopped what she was about to say. "You had no right! I was..." Then Kelton could see the anger come on as she stomped her foot and jabbed her finger into his chest. "One, you are not my man. Two, I can do whatever the **hell** I want or say. Three..." She took a deep breath and looked down at her boots. "They were the first boots I bought with my first big paycheck from modeling. The only thing I purchased that wasn't..." She waved her hand. "You know... Needed. I always save, only spend what I need, but these were the first thing I actually wanted and could buy."

Kelton sighed. "I'll give you the word, but I have every right Laney, because before this week is up you will be mine. In my bed, your body marked by me and needing me like you have never needed anything," he said, stepping close and softly placing a kiss on her lips."

Laney shook her head and tried to step back, but he held on.

"Oh no, you don't. There will be no running away. Now I promised you something pretty to see and I keep my word, always," he said.

Chapter Three

Laney didn't say a word as she allowed Kelton to escort her down the path. He led her to a breath-taking view of a waterfall, but her mind was screaming "nut job" and told her that she needed to get away.

The man sighed and leaned against a large bolder, releasing her for the first time they had made it down there. "I am the oldest of four that will be here tomorrow. No, my father is not crazy. But when we do find someone that we connect to, we don't allow that person to get away. Maybe it's genetics since you are your mother's daughter. Who knows?" The man scanned her from head to toe.

"How could you know this? You don't even believe my story. No, I just need to grab my bag and go home. It's obvious my mother hasn't changed. She still lies." Laney glanced out at the waterfall, anywhere but at him.

"I will never lie to you Laney, but I am a hard man to live with. I will expect to be listened to and I'm in a firm believer in using my hand, hairbrush or paddle to spank you if my rules are not followed. Some spankings can be for pleasure and some will be for punishment," he said, coming up behind her, wrapping his arms around her, scaring the hell out of her as she jumped.

"Relax, I'm not going to hurt you, Laney. I have a ranch in North Dakota. I raise buffalo, steers, chickens and other animals. Some I sell, others I send to places like the reservations to help them when times are hard. I also try and buy every wild horse I can, bringing them back placing them where they can reproduce. Too many of our animals are dying out and need to have a chance to grow again," Kelton said.

"You must have a very big place to have all that," she said, turning to look over her shoulder as she heard someone coming down the path. She sighed, seeing it wasn't in the cards for her to get away quickly, as Omar and her mother had joined them. Omar glanced at his son.

"Mine," Kelton said, holding on to her tightly, and that just pissed her off again.

"Excuse me? I am not yours and as soon as I am free, I'll be on the first plane back to New York," she growled and tried to get loose from his arms, but he held tight.

"She does have her mother's spirit. Talk to her now." Omar said, looking down at her mother.

"I'm sorry Laney. I hadn't informed anyone of my problems including Omar. I wanted to forget my past. I still have nightmares. It took me over two years to clean myself up after you left." Her mother said, glaring at Omar. "I wouldn't have called, but Omar believes family should be together for the holidays, that we should try and make an amends."

"So, let me get this straight. You wouldn't have even called me if it wasn't for Omar? You couldn't even care less how I faired? Or that you are sorry for trying to sell me? Let me go Kelton, now," she said, but he shook his head.

Using what she had been taught in self-defense class,

Laney dropped, spun and came up connecting with his cock. "Never underestimate me," she said and took off up the path as Kelton crumbled to the ground, growling.

Behind her Omar laughed, he actually laughed. "You better run far and fast daughter, because when he is feeling better he's going to tan your butt." Omar yelled.

Laney didn't even bother going into the house and just ran for the road. She'd catch a damn ride to the airport, charge her ticket to her account and forget about her bag in the house. Even though she did love the pair of jeans she'd packed away.

Slowing down, Laney made it to the end of the drive, and started to make her way down the road to the diner where she'd call Taz. She'd call the taxi and make the plane ride all the while yelling at her, I told you so.

She snorted, shaking her head, taking a deep breath. What Laney wasn't expecting was Kelton coming up behind her, grabbing her and throwing her over his shoulder as he headed back towards the house. His hand came down on her ass hard.

"Wait till I get you to your room," he growled.

"Put me down right now! You have no right," she said. Laney looked up and smiled as a cop pulled up, lights flashing.

"Stop right there plcase," The officer said and Kelton stopped, slowly dropping her to the ground, but holding onto her.

"Ma'am, are you okay?" he asked, coming around the car, but stopped, sniffing the air. "What is going on?"

Kelton's hold on her got tighter as her stepfather stepped next to them. "Sanders, it's good to see you. I'd like you to meet my eldest son Kelton. It seems he has met his woman and has started the bonding, I'm afraid."

"Bonding?" she said. " I'm not his anything. Damn it, I just met these people. All I'm doing is trying to get home," she hissed out.

"Cussing," Kelton growled, biting down on her ear lobe.

"Ma'am, I would ask that you allow this man to explain what is going on before anything else." The officer looked at Kelton. "You'll explain to her what is going before we get any more calls, OK?"

Kelton growled, behind her and when Laney looked up, she froze. His eyes now had gold flecks in them.

"Wow," she whispered.

He looked down at her and a chill went up her spine. "Please come back and allow me to explain what I mean. If you want to leave then... I'll drive you to the airport," Kelton growled.

Laney took a deep breath, looking back at the cop, who nodded. "Trust me when he explains everything, it will make sense." The cop walked around the car and turned off his lights. "Are we going to see you tonight?" he asked, but Omar who shook his head.

"No, I have my own problem to take care of," Omar said, looking back to the woods, and that is when Laney noticed her mother standing there, as a small whimper came out of her, but Laney had seen the glint of a smile as she lowered her head looking at the ground. Yes, her mother was not fooling her.

"Well, have a good night and hope to see all of you soon," the cop said as he got into his car.

Kelton held out his hand. Laney stared at it for a minute before placing her hand into his. She didn't say a word as they all headed back to the house.

Omar swept her mom up into his arms. "We'll have

110

dinner at eight," he said and Kelton nodded, leading her upstairs to the room Omar had shown her earlier.

"Please have a seat," Kelton said, removing his shirt and shoes.

"What are you doing?" Laney asked, plopping down on the ottoman. But then as she ogled his amazing abs, she thought, who was she to turn down looking at a hot shirtless man, but she also didn't want it leading anywhere right now.

"I'm going to show you something, then we will talk. Please don't run. I promise I won't hurt you and I know it's you when I change," Kelton said before he dropped to his knees. What had just moment's before been a handsome, but literally pain in the ass man was now a full grown gray wolf, with big green eyes and sharp teeth.

"Okay, now I'm going crazy," she muttered as the wolf growled, but sat down watching her. "Wow. I thought this trip was going to be wild, but this is way out there. Okay, change back and tell me why this matters," Laney said, curling up on the ottoman, as she watched him change back.

She swallowed, as he stood, completely naked, and thought, "My God, does he have a body!"

He reached down pulling his pants on coming over to her. He lifted her up and placed her on his lap, holding her.

"We are not crazy. I'm just different from you. A different species. There are many of us that others do not know about," he took a deep breath. "We do have different ways to do things. For instance, when we meet our other, both the wolf and human can scent the person meant to be theirs. I knew the minute I stepped into the house and saw you there on the stairs that you were meant to be mine." He placed a kiss on her cheek. "You see, the wolf and the man must both agree on a woman. Even before I saw you, I could smell you and the wolf was going crazy, wanting you."

Laney shook her head. "This is crazy. You should be with someone of your kind. Plus, this here is my mom's." Laney said, pointing to her surroundings. "I owe you an apology Kelton for what I did to you earlier, but when mom spoke it was like I was a child again. She knows how to say the right thing, and she still hurts the crap out of you. I hate to say this, because she is my mom, but I feel sorry for your dad if he's stuck with her."

Chapter Four

Kelton held onto Laney as she laid her head down on his chest. "Stay the week, Laney. Let us get to know each other. Who knows, maybe being with my father will change your mother." Kelton said, feeling the hurt emotions coming from his woman. "If not for your mom, give us a chance. This too isn't me, Laney. Let's take time to get to know each other."

She sat up and looked at him. "You're not going to let me go, are you?" she asked.

"No, if I had to follow you back to New York, I would. But I would hope you would give me a chance to prove to you that we belong together. I won't ever lie to you. Laney, I'm an alpha wolf and I expect my woman to be beside me." He leaned over and bit the bottom of her lip. "I will spank you, Laney. I'm a strong believer in punishment. But punishment can also be turned into pleasure. I personally can't wait to make a paddle just for you. How much experience do you have where it comes to sex?" he asked.

Laney glanced away, but he wouldn't allow, it putting a finger on her cheek, bringing her attention back to him. "Eyes on me."

"Not much, I've only been with one man. But really didn't have time to commit to a relationship with him. I needed to make sure I had enough money for a place to live and eat."

"My poor Laney, that is about to change." He lifted her up, placing her in front of him. "We'll start now. Strip for me, Laney. Let me see how beautiful you are. Then I'll start a nice warm bath for you, while I get my things," Kelton said, waiting.

He watched as she glanced at the door. "No one will come in here, honey. It's just you and me."
She looked at him and sighed, bending down to unzip her ruined boots.

Kelton promised her that he would find another pair for her, now knowing how much they had meant to her. One thing he had always thought was sexy was when a woman undressed for her man.

Right now, watching Laney, he could see the doubt and the fear, but trusting him enough to allow her blouse to drop to the floor was the sexist thing he had ever seen. Well second. Watching her wiggle out of her dress pants was the first.

His cock hardened and his wolf panted, but when she turned just a few inches, he stood. "Stop," he said, wrapping his arm around her, turning her so he could see the scar on her stomach.

Kelton ran his finger over the long scar. "This is why you are covered in most of your shots?" he asked, his homework on her background came in handy.

She lifted her chin. "Yes. I guess I could afford to have it fixed now, but it reminds me each day what could happen to me if I follow in my mother's shoes. I refuse to allow this to happen to me. Any child I have will have a mother who loves her and who would give up her own life for her."

Kelton pulled her into his arms, hugging her tight. "I was trying to decide what was sexier—you taking off your shirt, or the way you wiggled that cute ass taking off your pants. But once more I was wrong." He leaned back and cupped her cheeks. "Nothing compares to what you just said. Not only was it sexy as hell, but you have captured this alpha wolf with one statement. Sorry honey, I'm afraid you will never get rid of me. I know for a fact you will carry my children." He slid his hand down, placing it on her lower belly, where her the top of her sexy panties were.

He lowered his head, covering her mouth with his, sliding his tongue into her, claiming what was his. She trembled in his arms, as Laney brought her arms up and slid them around his neck, moaning as he showed her how to make love with just a kiss.

Kelton caressed, tasted and taught her how to play, dueling with their tongues, while he slid his hand in her shoulder-length hair, grabbing a handful of it, holding her head still.

"Well, it would seem you are like me in some ways," her mother said, breaking their moment. Kelton held on to Laney, when she would have moved away from him.

"You were not invited in this room and she's nothing like you. Leave now," he growled, putting Laney behind him just as his father ran into the room.

"I'm sorry Kelton, this shouldn't' have happened," his father glanced at his woman. "I've called your sisters and brother. They're all going to meet at your place for Thanksgiving dinner. Laney, I've also called your brother. He and your aunt will also be joining you there. My mate and I need a few more days. If things go well, we'll meet you at your place Kelton. I've called your second, Bass, and he is setting everything up, the rooms and such. I'm sorry son. Laney I had no idea."

Laney peeked around him. "It's not your fault. I honestly hope you can work things out, but after 28 years of being the same self-centered bitch..." Laney growled as her mother lunged for her, but his father snatched her up and threw her up over his shoulder, slapping her ass hard, turning to leave.

"Dad you can't... until you know." Kelton said.

"I know Kelton..." he said, leaving and shutting the door.

Kelton released the breath he was holding and turned to Laney.

"I know it was stupid, but I felt so sorry for your father," Laney sat down and shook her head, before looking up at him. "She'll lie, steal, do whatever she can." Laney frowned. "Are they already married?" she asked.

"No. Not bonded yet either, why?" he asked.

"Well, my aunt is a twin to my mother, but from what I've heard, she's nothing like mom," Laney laughed. "When I was small and I pissed mom off, she used to say I was just like her twin. Maybe your dad needs to be with her. Maybe at Thanksgiving dinner, your father can see."

Kelton helped Laney up and kissed her cheek. "Hop in the shower, I'll call the jet and have it ready. I don't know about your aunt, but I'll see if I can speak with my father before we leave," Kelton said, pushing her towards the bathroom.

He zipped up his pants, grabbing his shirt.

"Kelton?" Laney called from the bathroom doorway.

He turned to see her smile. "I won't forgive mom. She is dead to me now. This was her last chance and she blew it."

* * *

Laney stared out the window of the jet. When they had packed up the car, Omar had met them outside. He had hugged her and his son, apologizing again.

It seemed her mother was not his bonded one after all, and for that she was extremely grateful. After sending her mother to rehab, he would be joining them at Kelton's home. She really hoped her aunt was the one he was looking for, because Omar deserved to be happy too.

Laney did have to admit she didn't know how she felt about seeing her brother and aunt. She was already emotionally exhausted.

She leaned her forehead on the cool window, releasing the breath she'd been holding, closing her eyes.

"Here honey, drink this," Kelton said, handing her a shot glass.

"What is it?" she sniffed it. "Hmmm, is this bourbon?" She asked, swallowing the drink and smiling. "Yea, Evan Williams, right?"

Kelton's eyes heated up and he smiled. "Let me guess, you're a bourbon gal?" he said, laughing.

"Hell yeah. Sorry, but I'll always take a shot of bourbon over a glass of wine. Now, once in a while at night I might break down and have some Irish cream over some ice for a nightcap. Especially when it's been a rough day."

Kelton sat down beside her. "What would you consider a rough day?" he asked.

She snorted, seeing the doubt there in his eyes. Laney didn't hold it against him since so many didn't know what a day was like for a photo shoot. So, she proceeded to tell him letting him know that the day usually started at 4:00 in the morning and ended some days at 7:00 at night. By the time she finished, he was growling.

"I want names of every camera guy who touched or tried anything," Kelton demanded.

Laney laughed and reached over hugging him. "Thank you, you've made my day."

"I mean it, Laney. I will expect a list of those who dared cross the line. They shouldn't be in the business."

She shrugged. "You can take them out, but others will replace them and then no one will hire you because they are afraid you'll open your mouth. No, it's better to make sure you're never alone. Just do your job and no after-parties." She frowned. "But there is one name I will give you. He shouldn't be out there." She looked at him. "If you have any power, go find Jeff Davis. There was this little girl who was shooting with us one day…"

He reached over and squeezed her hand. "Don't, I'll take care of him, trust me." Kelton said. "Now, I need to warn you when we get home, and this is your home now, I have a few pets," Kelton said.

Laney turned and stared at him. "It better not be snakes or spiders. Or I will be staying at a hotel."

He laughed. "No, nothing like that. But I have an Irish wolfhound, Duke. He's the inside animal. Then there are my horses and my buffalo. I have two buffalo I nursed when they were babies. They kind of grew on me, so I kept them. Then there are my three wild horses I adopted. Two I can ride, the third nothing, but I won't give up on him."

Laney laughed. "You might be worth all the pain, Mr. Mason." she looked back out the window.

"Okay, why the long face? Your mother is being taken care of. Did your brother do something?" he growled.

"No, he wasn't there. He left when I was 14. Maybe it was the fact mom made him work and give her all his money while we had nothing. I don't know half of what she did. The last two years he was hardly home. He'd come home after school, hand me a bag of food before mom would get home, change clothes and leave. I'd always made sure to eat before she got home. To hide the food too. I forgot once, never again. One week I had no food except for what I got at school. So, I can't blame him for leaving." Laney said. "I just wish he would have taken me with him." She sighed.

"But I know I was a pest for him. What teenaged boy would take the responsibility of making sure I had at least one meal a day. He needed to break away. God knows what Mom would have done to him when he turned 18 with her acting crazier each day."

"I'm surprised your aunt didn't try and get you. I'm sure your brother had to tell her something," Kelton growled. "How old were you when you left?"

"Seventeen, I was lucky Taz was there when I got off that bus. If she hadn't stepped in, I would have been one of those hookers on the streets you see." Laney laughed. "You should have seen the two of us. Taz is 6'3," dark skin with big blue eyes. We were in Central Park one afternoon, just playing around.

Well, there happened to be a shoot in the park that day. An assistant to the photographer decided we were the perfect subjects, even though we didn't know he was taking pictures of us and the time and had no idea what we were signing when we signed the photo release. We didn't find out until two weeks later on when were on the front page of the *New York* magazine. We used our last $10 to buy the magazine. It seems they had been looking for us for the past week and a half, but we had given them fake cell phone numbers because we didn't have any phones. Needless to say, Taz and I received our first checks that day. We got our first apartment, well a hotel, until we could find a decent place to live. Oh, those first few weeks we had a ball looking for a place to live in New York. We finally found a basement apartment we rented from this couple. The rest you pretty much know."

"Excuse me, Mr. Mason your lunch order is ready," the stewardess informed them.

"Wow, what a spread and on a jet, talk about classy," she teased Kelton, but at once he frowned.

"I travel a lot, on business. Matter of fact, too much. If I had it my way I'd be on the ranch all the time. Didn't you travel for your shoots?" He asked, helping her up and escorting her to the table.

"Nope, Taz was deathly afraid of planes. It's one of the reasons she didn't want me to come. Plus, she knew what a psychotic witch mom was. Remember I told you we did everything together. I wasn't lying. We saw too many women getting hurt," Laney said as Kelton placed two huge sandwiches on her plate, potato salad and some kind of Jell-O thing.

"You know I can get my own food," Laney said.

"I know you can, but I would like to feed you, if you'd allow it?" He sat down beside her.

"Laney, as I said before, I'm not like normal males. I want to take care of you. Brush your hair, help pick out your clothes, sometimes feed you, and bathe you. I guess in some aspects I would say I'm kind of like what you human males called a Daddy Dom. I fully believe in discipline. We'll have toys to play with, but there is one thing I don't do." He cupped her cheek. "I don't share. I'm possessive, you're mine, mine only. Anyone who even thinks about touching or even looking at you sideways..." He growled so viciously that she had to do a double take. Sure enough, the gold specks in his eyes were there again. In some spooky way, it was sexy. Laney liked the idea of being his only. After so protecting herself for so long and fending for herself, well it excited her.

Chapter Five

Kelton swept Laney up before she could take two steps out of the limo that had been waiting for them at the airport.

"What are you doing? I can walk, or is this something else you're going to do for me? Because I have to tell you, I've always dreamed of having a man sweep me up in his arms," she said, laying her head on his shoulder, her arms wrapped around his neck.

"I'm carrying you over the threshold now, because once you enter my den, this big bad wolf will never let you go," he said, baring his teeth.

She giggled, placing a kiss on his cheek. "I like the sound of that, my big bad wolf, but I have to admit I can't wait to see you in a nice pair of tight jeans and a cowboy hat. Tell me, can you make love on a horse?" she teased as Bass opened the front door.

"Hell, yes you can, all sorts of ways," said another giant of a man. "Welcome home, Laney. The whole pack is excited that our alpha has found his woman finally," his best friend, Bass, said.

"Watch it, Bass," Kelton growled, not liking his friend talking to his woman about sex.

Bass held up his hands and moved out of the way as

Kelton's dog, Duke, sat there, his tail wagging, waiting to greet the new member of their family.

Kelton lowered her feet to the floor, worried that she would find his place too manly. "You can change anything you want," he said quickly, glancing at his pride and joy, the fireplace he had built, hopping she liked it.

"I wouldn't change a thing. Maybe add a few pillows, a picture here and there, but it's stunning. The fireplace is amazing." She knelt in front of Duke and held the palm of her hand out to him. "Hi there, big guy. Are we going to get along okay?"

Duke didn't even hesitate and began licking her hand and pushing her forward, knocking her backwards on her butt with his head. She laughed, laying there playing with Duke. "You're just a big baby, aren't you," she said placing a kiss on the top of his head.

"Duke family," Kelton said, kneeling down and giving him the command, even though he didn't think he needed to the way the two were carrying on. "Protect, Duke," he said, giving one more command.

"He's amazing, Kelton. I've always wanted a pet and now I'll have one."

Kelton smiled, watching the two of them. Glancing up, he saw Bass waiting and Kelton knew his friend was waiting for something.

"How would you like to take a sunset ride with me? I can show you the land, my other animals and we could even take a light supper since we ate a late lunch?" he asked. Seeing her eyes light up, Kelton knew he had said the right thing.

"Let me change into some jeans," she frowned. "But I don't have any boots. All I have is tennis shoes and dress shoes."

"Put on your tennis shoes. I'll carry you to the barn. I'm going to have the boys get my horse ready. I'll be back in a minute," he said.

Laney smiled and stood on her tippy toes, kissing his chin. "I know Bass has been waiting to tell you something." She patted his chest. "Just point me in the way to the bedroom and my suitcase," she said.

"Crap, I forgot it, hold on." He ran outside, growling seeing his ex, Red, sniff around the limo.

"So, it's true, you found your mate?" she asked, looking around him to the doorway where Kelton knew Laney stood, watching.

Duke growled behind him, never liking Red.

"I wouldn't move Red. You know he's trained to kill," Kelton said. "Laney, please get in the house. The master bedroom is the last door down the hallway. Wait for me there, now," he growled.

Laney rolled her eyes, moving into the house, muttering something respect. "Kelton. Don't you dare hurt her. I'd be pissed too if you showed up with someone else if I were dating you. Maybe you should have called her when you found out I was your mate, no?" she said, slamming the front door.

Kelton was speechless. He never imagined his woman would speak to him like that.

"Well, that's some woman you got there, Kelton." Red said, shaking her head.

I was prepared to hate her, but…" Red said, glancing at the door. "Where's the mom now?" Red asked.

"On the way to a permanent rehab."

Kelton couldn't believe he was having this conversation with her and that they had avoided a fight.

"Laney was right, I should have called and

personally informed you. I'm hoping eventually you two will hit it off. She's going to need a friend in the pack to watch her back," he said as Bass came out.

"There's been four females sniffing around from Thor's pack," Bass said.

Red growled as he did. "They're looking for information," Red said, "But don't worry. I'll watch her back and so will the others. They're not going to allow the riff raff to stir up trouble here," Red said, heading towards her car.

"Red, come to dinner on Thanksgiving. I want you and Laney to talk," he called out to her. She gave him the finger.

He snorted. "I swear, where is the respect," he grumbled, but laughed. "Dinner is sure going to be lively." Kelton headed to the door. "Bass, have my horse ready. We'll be down in 30 after I show my lovely woman what it is like to be spanked."

Bass laughed, heading towards the barn, doing what was asked of him.

The thought of having Laney naked over his knees had Kelton's cock stretching painfully in his pants. But unfortunately, this punishment was not a fun one.

She stared out the window when he moved into the room closing the door. He placed her suitcase on one side of the bed, sitting on the other.

"Come here, Laney," he said, waiting.

She stood there for a second, before coming to stand between his legs. "For the record, I wouldn't have hurt her and she wouldn't have hurt you. I was afraid that if you and she got into a fight, she might have bitten you and started your change, which we'll go into later, but you disrespected back there. Strip Laney, you've earned your first punishment. You should have let me handle this first incident," he told her, waiting to see what she would do.

"But…" Laney bit her bottom lip, before looking at the window.

Kelton watched her struggle with what he was asking. He knew once she did this, there would be no going back. Laney would be his totally, spanking and all.

A single tear rolled down her cheek as she stepped back and proceeded to strip and place herself over his lap. Never had he been given such a gift in his life. He ran his hand over her large white globes. "I thank you Laney for the gift and I promise I will always protect and love you."

Kelton brought down his hand on her skin followed by six more. Laney tried to get up, but he held her down. "Let it go, Laney. I'm here, baby girl. No one is going to hurt you. You're safe," he said, spanking her three more times on both cheeks, till Laney let loose.

She cried and cried as he lifted her up, holding on to her, knowing his Laney was crying for all the pain of her childhood, the loneliness she's suffered, the abuse. All of it came out, as she buried her face into his neck crying, but holding onto him tight as if afraid he was going to leave.

"I'm here, Laney. You will never be alone again. Someone would have to kill me before I left you, my baby girl." He held her, allowing her to gather herself as a few of his own tears joined hers. The thought of little Laney alone and by herself as a child hurt him too. He had been protected by his family, but what he was feeling now scared him, because he knew he'd kill without a thought if someone…

Laney lifted her head, her eyes big, as she reached up, wiping his tears. "You cry for me?" she asked.

"Yes, I cry for the little girl inside who still needs someone to take care of her. Maybe that is why the fates have brought us together. My need to protect, care for you and love you, like no one ever has or could."

Laney cuddled up on him. You know how I knew you were the right one for me?" She asked, kissing his chest.

"How?" he asked, rubbing her arms, taking in her scent so his wolf would always know how to find her.

"When you were talking about your animals. I could see the love there, even though they were different, that's how we fit. I'm tired of having to do it all, Kelton. I just want to be held and not have to worry when I'm going to eat next or where I'm going to sleep."

He lifted her up and set her at the end of the bed. "Get dressed, baby girl. We have a sunset to watch, a picnic to eat, and I'm going to show you how a cowboy makes love to his woman on his horse." He growled, cupping her breast and squeezing it.

"Really?" Laney said, running around the bed, but stopped. "Don't you think it would be easier if I wore a skirt if we're going to make love on the horse?" she asked.

"Jeans. Are you questioning me already?" he growled and stepped forward.

"No," she squeaked, throwing her clothes around pulling her jeans out.

"No underwear or a bra either," he snarled, wanting to pounce, but holding himself back. Tonight, he would show her how a man loved his woman.

Chapter Six

Laney had never laughed so hard as when Kelton carried her to the barn and then slipped on a pile of cow or horse shit. Oh, Kelton made sure she never got hurt, but he had landed smack in the pile of shit.

Slapping her butt for laughing at him, Kelton deposited her into the barn before turning around and going back into the house to change his clothes. Laney put the picnic basket down and moved into the barn, peeking in the stalls at all the horses and animals till her phone rang.

Cussing up a storm, Laney took out her phone, seeing Taz's number. "Hey pretty lady, what's going on? I thought you'd be on your way to supreme boyfriend's home." Laney said, reaching out and patting the most beautiful horse she had seen.

"He never showed up. He's gone Laney, and so is my money. I trusted him," Taz cried.

"What? We'll find him and then I'll feed him to the wolves, literally," she said, smiling as Kelton moved up to her, wrapping his arms around her.

"What's wrong, little girl?" he asked, nibbling on her neck.

"Do you mind one more for Thanksgiving? It seems

Taz's so called boyfriend had wiped out her bank account and left her."

"What? Let me talk to her, Laney," Kelton said, holding out his hand.

"Taz, I'm going to put my man on the phone. I'll explain when you get here, trust him Taz," Laney said, giving him the phone.

"Taz, this is Kelton. I'm going to send my brother to swing by and pick you up since he has decided to drive here. I want you to pack enough for a few weeks. It would give you time to rest and decide what you want to do next. Do you have access to a computer?" he asked. "Good, send me an email with everything about this man that took your stuff and I promise we'll get everything back. My brother's name is Samuel Mason. Now, I'll give you back to Laney." He turned to Laney. "I'll get the horse ready," he said, placing a kiss on her cheek and walking down the barn.

"Hey Kelton, whose horse is this?" Laney asked.

Kelton smiled. "That is my wild lady. The one I told you about."

"She's stunning," Laney said. "I'm back, Taz. Now, do as Kelton said and get your butt here. I really think you are going to love it here. I have so much to tell you." She peeked and saw that Kelton was way down at the other end. "Taz, he's the one, everything like we talked about."

"What? You mean, the man?" Taz asked. "How did you meet him?" She asked.

"He was going to be my stepbrother, but lucky for his father, that didn't turn out. Mom's finally in rehab. Please come, you're my family and I want you here to meet Kelton." Laney begged and watched as Kelton led his horse to her.

She did have to admit the man had the best ass in

jeans, and the way he wore his cowboy hat partly covering his eyes, so she couldn't guess what he was thinking sent a chill up her spine.

"I'll be there. I can't wait to meet 'the man.' Do you want me to pack more of your stuff? Are you going to stay there a while?" she asked.

"Tell her not to worry about your things. We'll all go back later when things get settled after the holidays. It will give Taz time to decide what she wants too, because she's welcome to stay here till she decides what she wants," Kelton said before Laney could say anything.

"How did you...You heard?" she squeaked.

"Oh, baby girl, big bad wolves had excellent hearing and I can't wait to hear what your 'the man' is all about. We will be discussing that over diner," he said, with the voice that sent a chill down her spine.

"Wow, he's good. Damn, even my nipples hardened. You lucky bitch," Taz said.

"You know you don't sound so upset about Max," Laney said.

"I'm not. When you left I really took a look at what we had. I was going to break it off Laney, he didn't give the chill. Didn't want..." Taz stopped.

"You'll find the right man, but until then let Kelton help you find Max. Believe me, he'll get your money back. Now I'll see you in a few days. Expect his brother?" she asked.

"Tomorrow. I'll have him call her when he's close," Kelton came over and scooped her up, placing her on his horse.

"Why he's huge. Taz, I'll see you in a few days. Love you, lady" Laney said, hanging up her phone and putting it in Kelton's hand as he waited for it.

"I didn't know you had brought that with you," he said, giving her a look.

She shrugged. "It's another promise we made to each other. We'd keep our phone on us at all times in case something happened to the other."

He slid the phone into the picnic basket, handing it to her, before getting up behind her. "I can see why you did it and I'm proud of you for taking such precautions. So, you like Wild Lady? I'll tell you what, she's yours, but you will wait till I make sure she's safe to ride before you even go into that stall," Kelton said, placing a kiss on her neck, guiding his horse out of the barn and out into the pasture.

She took a deep breath; the air was getting cool. "You know it might be a little cool to have a picnic and make love outside," Laney said. "You guys are lucky you haven't had any snow yet. I have to admit I love when we have an Indian summer. You can still scent all the fall smells, but be warm."

"I see I have my work cut out for me, proving that I will take care of you." Kelton bit down on her neck pointing to the right releasing her neck. "Look, they've come to great us," Kelton said.

"You keep biting me and I'm going to be covered in your marks, or is that the idea. I know my ass has your hand print on it," she grumbled and tried to move.

"Soon, not only will your ass will be warm but your pussy. Have you ever had it spanked?" he asked, stopping the horse, jumping down before turning to help her down. "In the basket I packed some carrots for these two buffalos. The one on the left with the white mark on his face is Owl, and his sister I call Tangerine, because she is the sweetest thing I've ever seen." Kelton ran his hand over Tangerine's head. "How are you doing, momma?" he said. "She's pregnant with twins."

"They are beautiful, Kelton." Laney gave him a carrot as she fed the male, Owl. "Will you keep her calves?" she asked.

"Yes. These two are the best stock I've had. Owl there has a few of his own little ones running around in the pasture over there to the left. I eventually plan to fill my pastures with buffalo. The meat is healthier and there are many uses for the hide, but these two will live their lives here." Kelton said.

"Well, I have to say I'm impressed. I have to agree. I've had buffalo a few times. I'd like to go with you when you deliver the buffalo to the tribes. There are so many that don't have anything. I have tried to donate to a few of the schools, helping with coats, materials and such." Laney pulled her coat around her as the wind started to pick up.

"Come, we have little ways to go," Kelton said lifting her back up on the horse, hitting her sore butt.

"Should have brought a damn cushion," Laney mumbled.

"Punishment wouldn't be a punishment if it didn't hurt, Lane," Kelton said, climbing in behind her and guiding his horse out towards the valley.

"I've told Bass we wouldn't be back. We're going to be staying the night out here. There will be no interruptions. Tomorrow we'll go back and start getting things ready for our guests," Kelton said as he started pointing out different areas to her, making sure Laney knew where to go if she ever got lost out here.

Twenty minutes later Kelton stopped in front of a small cabin.

Next to the cabin was a large building that was so out of place. "What is that?" she asked, as he picked her up, taking the basket off the horse.

"That is my private area. I have a few horses out here I break away from all the noise. Eventually I'll bring Wild lady out here. The only ones that comes out here are a few hands, but I've sent them all home, so we have this place to ourselves." He guided her to the side of the house where a big bonfire was going in a stone fire pit on the deck of the house. There were blankets and a bottle of something in a bucket of ice.

"My God, this is beautiful, Kelton," Laney said, tears filling her eyes as she looked out at the hills around them. "You did this all for me?" she asked.

"I'll always take care of you, Laney. Now strip, Laney, you'll be warm enough here behind the fire. I want to be able to touch and play with you while we eat, watching the sunset," he told her pointing to the blankets, all ready for them.

She looked around, and knew no one would be out here. Stripping out of her clothes, Kelton joined her, leaving his pants on, but unzipping them as he pulled her down on the blanket and that is when she found out the blankets were heated.

"I hope we can do this often," Laney said as Kelton pulled her into his lap. "Are you hungry now? Or do you want to wait?" he asked.

She turned to face him, sliding her arms around his neck. "Later, I'd like to explore what I have here," Laney said. "We do have a few minutes before the sun will set." She loved his hair, it was thick and dark against her skin as she ran her hands through it, freeing it from his tie. "I don't know how I lucked out. I have to say you are one fine looking male, Mr. Mason." She leaned down placing kisses on his shoulder to his neck. "And you always smell so good."

He growled and turned her around so she faced away from him. "You can touch later. I'm too close and I want to explore before I bury myself in you," he said, placing both of her legs back on the side of his legs, spreading her open.

"Now, watch the sun set Laney, while I play," he pulled her arms up. "Wrap your arms around my neck and keep them there."

"But…" she didn't get any more out as Kelton slapped her pussy lips, not only shocking her, but exciting her.

"Quiet, you'll get your time, but later, baby girl," he spanked her pussy lips three more times, before reaching behind him, under the blanket and pulling out a clear glass dildo. "Um, nice and warm and you are soaking wet," he said, sliding the tip up and down her lips, before sliding it in and out of her slowly.

"Kelton," she whispered resting her head back on his shoulder.

"That's it baby, relax just feel," he said his other hand covering her breast squeezing as he loved her with the warm glass toy. It was long and a little thick, but it felt so good.

Hell, she should have known he'd keep her warm. Laney was burning up, as he increased the movements before pushing the toy all the way in and spanking her pussy with it in her. "God!" Laney whimpered.

"You can come anytime you want. Tonight, I plan to show you every different way spankings can enhance your sexual pleasure. Do you know how beautiful you are right now? The sun going down, your skin flushed, your nipples hard and the scent of your excitement has me barely hanging on here. Listen, do you hear it?" he asked, reaching over again under the blanket pulling out a little black button.

Click's pierced the night, the kind of a photographer taking pictures. "That's right baby girl. Bass set up my camera. I want pictures of my baby in the throes of passion," he said. "But we have a few more things to add to your photo shoot." He said, laying down the button and reaching under the blanket pulling out what looked like earrings. "I found these last year and knew I had to have them. I've saved them just for you," he told her taking one and screwing it on her nipple.

Laney had never had nipple clamps on before. Hell all of this was pretty new, but it would seem her man would be showing her many new pleasures as the pain had her squawking and wanting to grab on to her boob. "That hurt," she glared at him, earning another two smacks on her pussy, hard.

"Never give me that look, baby girl," he growled and bit down where her neck and shoulder met, holding her still as he proceeded to thrust the toy in and out of her, flicking the nipple clamp at the same time.

"Kelton!" she cried out as her body shook, pleasure shooting through her quick and hard when he stopped, taking the other clamp and putting it on her other nipple. Laney couldn't even form words as the pain seemed to just send another tremor through her.

"Let go of my neck and lean forward," he said, pushing her forward and down. He ran his hand over her sore ass, squeezing her cheeks. "Your body is beautiful. It's going to take me a lifetime to accomplish all the things I want to do to you. But first we're going to stretch this other little hole." He growled as something warm thin slid into her ass.

"Kelton," she cried out.

"Easy, this is just lube getting you ready," he said, pulling the tube out as the warm gel squirted in her. He worked one, then two of his fingers into her ass.

Laney held onto the blanket, as he removed his fingers, replacing it with something else, wider. "This is a small plug, you'll keep this in you tonight while I make love to you," he informed her while working the plug into her. "God, you look beautiful," he said, moving the plug in and out, twisting it before lifting her up back up and taking the glass toy out, before scooting back and standing.

She looked over her shoulder to see him strip out of his jeans. He was huge, just huge. Laney leaned over and licked the underside of his cock, earning a growl.

"Don't," he said, grabbing a handful of her hair, moving back behind her.

"Watch the sun set," he said, lifting her up and slowly worked his cock inside her. "So damn tight and mine," he growled, releasing her hair and grabbing onto her breasts as he slowly, started to move in and out of her.

Laney stared out as the sun moved down over the horizon, her body burning up with pleasure as her man held onto her, whispering to her how proud he was to have her in his arms. That she would never have to worry about a place to live or having enough to eat again.

Tears rolled down her cheeks, his kisses against her skin, his whispered words like fingers across her skin as she rose higher and higher, while the sun lowered. In all her life Laney would never forget this moment as the sun disappeared and her body shattered, when he reached down, rubbing her clit.

"That's it, come!" Kelton growled, his strokes powerful and fast as she swore fireworks were shooting all around her. His warm seed, filling into her, her legs shaking, her breath coming in gasps as Laney tried to control herself, but he wouldn't allow it, biting down once more, hard, breaking the skin and growling.

She felt the blood roll down her breast, but nothing mattered as her body was out of control, pleasure rippled through her, her screams echoing in the valley. Laney didn't know how long she had been out of it, but when Kelton removed the nipple clamp she jerked to attention and tried to grab her boob.

"Shit," she hissed, but her hand was pushed away as Kelton sucked her nipple into his mouth. Laney was lying on the blanket and he was over her, staring up at her.

"Welcome back, baby girl. You scared me there for a moment. For that alone, I should spank your butt," he growled.

Laney frowned as he helped her up. "I passed out?" she asked and he nodded, reaching over and removing the other clamp. "God! What are you, a sadist?" Laney grumbled and he laughed, removing her hand, sucking her nipple into his mouth.

"Hardly," he said, reaching again under the blanket and pulling out what looked like a big flannel nightgown, and sliding over her head. "I don't want you getting chilled as we eat."

Laney shook her head as he stood putting on his jeans and getting the picnic basket joining her again. "You really are going to take care of me?" she asked as he sat down next to her.

"Yes, Laney, I'm really going to take care of you," he leaned over licking her neck. "I've started the change, baby girl. Soon you will be fully mine, wolf and all. Tell me, do you want to continue to model with your friend Taz?" he asked, handing her a mug. "Chicken noodle soup to heat you up," he said.

"No, I've wanted to get out of modeling for a while. Always worrying about what you eat, how you look and such. Maybe I'll go back to school, do something online. I have time and money." She smiled. "You know Taz and I always talked about opening our own store. A sort of coffee shop bookstore. We both love to read. Is there a bookstore in town here?" she asked.

Kelton took a sip of his soup frowning. "You know I don't think so and the only place people go to get coffee around here is the fast food places. You know there is a little property at the intersection to the major highways that would be perfect for that. The building is big enough that you could make it what you want and it's not far from here," he said.

"I'd like that" she asked leaning over and taking a bite of the strawberry, he held up for her.

"I'd like to buy this property for the two of you. My gift to you two for starting your new adventure and lives," he said.

Laney smiled and stared at the man before her. Sure, she was nervous about meeting the rest of his family, but ever since she had stepped foot on this property and into his arms, Laney had come home. Spankings and all. "You know I wouldn't have cared if you were my stepbrother. I would have still fallen in love with you."

She Has To Touch
By Jennifer Williams

She had to touch. It had been a compulsion since she was young. Looking wasn't ever good enough. She needed to feel; the fur of a woman's coat, her mother's perfume bottles, the fancy electronics in the department store early on a Saturday morning. These things were her catnip. Never mind the scolding. Never mind being grounded. She *had* to touch.

The museum was her favorite place, precisely because it was forbidden here. You could look, but you weren't supposed to touch. She'd stood, often, in front of the lush paintings of seascapes and portraits, face so close she could see each tiny brushstroke. But she knew if she reached out, if she actually laid even one tiny finger on the canvas, a guard would come and scold her.

That was how she'd met Jonathan. She'd seen him, of course. He stood in stark contrast to the other security guards that worked there. In a job filled mostly by retirees, a young man stood out. But it wasn't just that. It was the way he looked at the pieces the museum held, as though he wondered, sincerely, as to the stories behind them. He intrigued her from the start.

The first time had been an accident. She'd been

leaning over to get a closer look at a cabinet inlaid with Mother of Pearl. She hadn't even noticed the sensors on the floor. The alarm sounded, an insistent beeping like the kind in a home security system, and Jonathan had come, his tall frame taking long strides. She'd stepped back, expecting to be admonished, or worse, kicked out. As soon as she had done so the alarm ceased its noise.

"Careful," he'd said, a small smile playing across his lips. "There're sensors in the floor." He pointed and she saw them.

The second time had not been an accident. She'd made sure he was working that night before slipping behind a rope to touch a gown stitched tight with pearls. It was heavy in her hands and she'd wished she could feel it against her naked skin, had wondered if it would hurt to lie upon it, each iridescent globe biting into her tender flesh as someone pressed down upon her. Jonathan had found her just as her eyes were fluttering closed. She hadn't even known his name then. But she knew his voice, had memorized it from that very first encounter.

"You're not supposed to do that," he'd said, voice closer than it ought to have been.

"I know."

She'd let the dress slip slowly from her hands, reluctant to let it go.

When she'd turned, she saw him watching her with such intensity that she'd nearly dropped to her knees right then.

Instead, she'd asked him his name. And he asked for hers. From there a sort of friendship had blossomed. Small talk mostly: the weather, idle chatter about work, occasionally discussions about the exhibits. He'd asked her once if she'd be attending one of the upcoming after-hours parties and it wasn't till she'd gotten home that night that she'd realized his face had fallen ever so slightly when she'd said no.

Now Riley stood before the extravagant Moon Bed, a gift to the Americas from China in the 1800's. That didn't really matter to her though. What mattered was the wood. Intricately carved and inlaid with ivory, it was just *begging* to be touched.

Her fingers twitched. She could see the sensors on the floor. She knew if she stepped too close an alarm would go off. Riley took a step closer, fingers reaching.

"I wouldn't."

Jonathan. She could feel his breath on her ear when he spoke.

She turned to face him. She'd never been this close to him before. His body dwarfed hers and she spared a quick glance around the exhibit hall. They were alone as far as she could tell.

"I was just looking…" she said.

Jonathan regarded her, eyes dark, and she felt her pulse quicken under his gaze.

A long moment passed with neither of them speaking. It might have been awkward but Riley could feel something shifting in the air between them. This was her opportunity. She'd imagined him so many times since that night he'd asked her about the party. She wanted to see his black hair let loose around his pale face, preferably while they fucked. She'd thought, often, of how his name would sound leaving her lips as she came. Had wondered, too, if he could be rough in just the way she liked it.

Now was as good a time as any to find out.

Riley stepped one foot back.

The alarm sounded.

Jonathan's eyes flashed in the bright lights of the exhibit.

"Am I in trouble?" she asked. Her voice shook faintly as she spoke.

He leaned in closer. "Yes," he whispered.

The way he said it, the way his voice dropped combined with the closeness of his body, his scent washing over her, made Riley's head swim. It held such promise.

"Go upstairs. Now," He said, taking a step away from her.

She was about to protest but then she heard it: the heavy footfall of another guard. The alarm was still sounding. She hadn't even noticed.

"Everything all right here?" the other security guard asked, a portly man with graying hair.

Riley smiled her sweetest smile. "Just me being clumsy," she replied as she walked away.

The alarm fell silent in her absence.

* * *

She walked aimlessly among the upstairs galleries. This was her least favorite section. Pottery and dinnerware and tiny porcelain figurines lined the walls in cabinets lit from within. The carpet was a god-awful shade of blue and chandeliers hung from the ceiling and she couldn't help but feel she was intruding in someone's home. Out of all the exhibits this one held the least appeal for her. It felt cold and nothing here invited her touch.

It was getting late. She could see that night had fallen outside and she wondered if Jonathan had forgotten about her. The museum would be closing soon. She was heading back towards the stairs when she heard him. He cleared his throat, alerting her to his presence, and she turned to find him standing in front of what she had assumed was a utility closet.

"I'm supposed to be sweeping this floor for guests," he said. One of his hands toyed idly with his belt buckle and Riley watched, captivated.

"We don't have much time," he continued. He took a step towards her, breaking her from her spell.

"Do you want this?" he asked. His voice was low and filled with unmistakable desire, and Riley felt it hit the pit of her stomach.

This was it. It was going to happen. But only if she wanted it to.

"Yes," she whispered. She swayed, overwhelmed by the prospect of what was to come, and he was on her in an instant, large hands holding her face, steadying her, forcing her to look at him.

"Tell me," he insisted. "Tell me **exactly** what you want."

She was losing it, she could tell. Her mind already propelled forward to the space her body would soon occupy. "Belt," was all she could push out for words, hoping he would understand.

He kissed her. A hard and bruising kiss that turned soft in its last few seconds and Riley found herself grabbing a fistful of his regulation dress shirt, pulling him closer.

"Not here," he said. He took her hand, entwining their fingers, and led her towards the door he'd been leaning against and it seemed so at odds with what they were about to do; a sweet gesture before a storm of violent pleasures.

"What is this place?" she asked. It was clearly not a

utility closet. They'd entered a dimly lit hallway. At the end of it was an old-fashioned service elevator, the kind with a folding metal gate, and there were stairs leading both up and down.

"We'll be safe here, but not for long." He pinned her against the railing, at the end leading up so there was no danger of her falling. "I cannot be gentle."

She felt his erection through his pants pressing against her. He wanted this, as much as she did. Maybe more.

"Do you agree?" he asked. He was breathless and desperate, just like her.

She nodded. Her cunt was already throbbing.

"Say it," he ordered, spittle flecking his lips, his sweetness turned sharp in the dark, with his hands hard upon her.

Riley barely gasped out "I agree," before he turned her, bent her over, and reached under her dress, yanking her panties down so roughly that the fabric bit into her skin and she heard some of the stitching tear.

"Fuck," she heard him say as he lifted the dress to look at her.

It was a sin, she knew, to like such things, to desire pain the way others desired tenderness. She had tried to be "good." Had dated men that had held her as though she were spun glass still warm to the touch. A thing to be molded into shapes they understood. But it had never worked and it had never ended well. This was what she wanted. To be on fire in their veins. To be consumed until she was nothing but ash, born anew with each mark upon her. Jonathan could give her that. Or so she hoped.

He squeezed one globe of her ass, sharp nails digging into her skin.

He kneaded each cheek in turn, before resting his

still caged cock between them and pulling her to him.

"Do you have any idea what you do to me?" he asked. But his voice was quiet. It was not a question she was meant to answer.

He held her there for a moment, no words, no movement. Only his hands holding her tight and his rigid cock pressed against her. In her mind, Riley saw them in a bed, naked and wild. Him, behind her. Nails raking red lines down her back. Her, face buried in a pillow, arms bound as he took her. Her hair would be a knotted mess from hours of play and he would be relentless, entering her without mercy.

She must have made a sound then; a moan, a sigh, a whimper. It didn't matter.

In an instant she felt his absence, stark and yawning like a chasm.

'Jon-"…

Thwack!

The sound was thunder, echoing through the hallway, and she jumped as his hand met her ass.

He hit her again, one hand on her back, steadying her, and she relaxed.

This. This was what she wanted.

One. Two. Three.

His hands were large and he was strong. Her skin grew warm under his punishment and she could easily picture the pink blush blooming there.

He fell into a rhythm, alternating between each globe, pausing occasionally to squeeze and pull at her ample flesh.

It was good. But it wasn't quite enough.

Each pain has its own flavor. And each, its own offering. Spanking was a dull sort of pain. It was thudding, dry and heavy. It made her think of rainy days, of clouds burdened, grey and roiling and ready to burst.

Riley wanted the storm, the flash of lightning promised in his eyes as he'd stared her down.

His hand continued to fall, beating the drum of her thighs and buttocks. But as the sound of skin striking skin echoed through the museum's hidden stairs, Riley grew silent and still.

By now she could recognize the arc of his body, the way his hip would turn against her own as he readied to swing. It was in this motion that he paused, his breath coming louder and faster than her own.

She worried that perhaps he'd misunderstood and mistaken her stillness for a lack of desire, or worse, boredom. Neither were true.

She was about to say something, about to reassure him, when he spoke.

'Belt," he said.

Riley smiled.

She wanted so badly to turn and look when she heard him releasing it and pulling it through the loops of his pants. Nothing got her wetter than watching a man taking a leather belt from around his waist, but she had little time to think on this as the first blow hit her, stinging and sharp like a razor.

The sound echoed through the hallway and Riley cried out. Her hands grabbed onto the banister instinctively. This was real. This wasn't a few light spanks administered with nervous laughter followed by a standard fuck. He was really going to…

"Ow!" He'd hit her again. No warning and no holding back. Her skin smarted where the leather had bit into it and she hoped she'd have bruises the next day.

She felt his free hand snake into her hair and pull.

"Can you be quiet?" he asked.

She didn't know if she could, but she didn't want him to stop.

She tried to nod but then she remembered. "Y-yes," she stuttered.

He held her like that, hand fisted in her hair as he administered three more blows in quick succession. Each one made her pussy quiver and she knew if he kept it up she'd come. She pushed her ass out expectantly to meet the next kiss of the belt but was met only with the cool air of the stairwell.

"So eager," he said as he laid the strap across her back, releasing her hair. "Don't move."

She felt him kneel behind her, wondered if she'd misjudged. Maybe he did just want to fuck. She expected to feel his tongue next, probing her, preparing her.

Instead, he bit her.

"Fucking hell," she whispered, her grip on the banister tightening.

He bit her ass, both cheeks of it. Not love bites. Not gentle. There would be bruises. Maybe even blood.

"Jonathan," she begged, her clit pulsing in time with her heartbeat.

He bit her once more before rising and taking the belt in his hand.

The next strike was pain, utter and exquisite. She heard him grunting with the effort; one, two, three more times. He didn't hold back and neither did she.

Her body shook as she came and she cried out. Not his name, like she'd imagined. She was too far gone for that. But a sound that was distinctly one of pleasure. She pulsed with need in that moment, wanting so badly for him to fill her.

He spun her round, seeming to sense what she desired, and kissed her deeply as his fingers found her wet and wanting.

"There's a new exhibit coming next week," he said, his lips hovering above hers, breath hot.

He moved slow and deliberate within her, pressing that spot just inside that always sent her reeling. Riley moaned as she rode his hand, hips pressing down, hands gripping him tight.

"Sculptures from India," he continued, fingers sliding out to rub her clit.

Riley trembled.

"Carved from stone," he said. He kissed her again, lightly, tongue tracing her lips before nipping tenderly. "Made smooth, like you." His fingers sank back into her, rhythm slow and steady and driving her wild.

She was panting and ready to come again, belly on fire and ass stinging as it pressed into the rails of the banister behind her.

"I know you like to touch," he said. He tapped his finger against the spongy spot just inside and her muscles tightened in response.

Riley felt herself unraveling.

"God, Riley," Her name sounded like worship on his lips.

She couldn't bring herself to care that he seemed to slip in that last moment from disciplinarian to supplicant.

His free hand slid down to cup her ass, fingernails raking across her raw skin.

"Will you come?" he asked, voice shaking.

But it was too late. She already was.

Punishment Befitting the Crime
By D.L. King

"Mr. Grant, these books are late. That's the second time this month you've had late returns and two of them have waiting lists."

The librarian's desk sat inside a circular granite enclosure with a marble counter top running all the way around, with the exception of an open entryway at the back leading into the office beyond. It was raised, making everyone who came to the desk feel small.

Ted Grant's hopes were rewarded; the head librarian was on duty tonight.

"I'm sorry Miss Carmichael but I had to work late every night this week. I didn't mean..."

"That's '*Mizz* Carmichael' and I don't want to hear any excuses." She looked down at him over her black, horn-rimmed glasses, her blue-black hair in a severe bun at the nape of her neck, the point of a pencil tapping its staccato rhythm on a ledger page.

"But I..."

"Silence!" she whispered. She thumbed through the ledger. "You've had late returns at least once every month for the past, let me see, seven months."

Ted got out his wallet. It was beginning to feel like

he was supporting the library single handedly. "How much do I owe?"

"Oh, I'm afraid you've gone beyond the *fine* stage. Come around to the door marked *No Admittance*."

It seemed the rumors might actually be true. Ted had been working on finding out for himself for quite a while now. He'd been diligently bringing books back late ever since that friend of Frank's had brought it up at the poker game. He'd said "That bitch of a head librarian punishes guys who break the library rules." He'd said that he heard she'd actually spanked some guy for bringing his books back late. He'd said it like it was a *bad* thing. Everybody laughed and made lewd remarks. That was all right; they weren't library types. He'd have been surprised if they read much more than the back of the cereal box or the sports page.

But he couldn't stop thinking about it. He began to fantasize about what kinds of punishments Ms. Carmichael might mete out to guys who didn't follow the rules—and now he was going to find out.

He walked around the desk and fidgeted as he waited for her to open the door. He felt like a little boy who'd been sent to the principal's office with the exception that a trip to the office in elementary school had never produced a hard-on. He crossed his hands in front of him just as the door opened and Ms. Carmichael, red lips pursed, gave him her most severe look yet. She led him to an office behind the desk.

"Sit here, Mr. Grant." She pointed to an old-fashioned hard-backed wooden chair. "It's late and I have to close the library. Don't move and don't touch anything."

"Yes, Ma'am."

He listened as the clicking of her high heels on the

tile floor receded. He fidgeted on the chair, adjusting himself. The office smelled of books and library glue mixed with a faint trace of perfume and… was that *sex*? It must be his imagination, he thought. His pants had become uncomfortably tight.

The sound of her heels grew louder until the door opened again. "Come with me," she said, and led him out the back door of the office and down a dingy hall, into the bowels of the library. He followed behind, mesmerized by her bottom, in its tight confinement, swaying from side to side until she stopped him at another door. "This is my special place for dealing with bad boys who flaunt the library rules," she said. His cock twitched in his pants. She looked at him pointedly. "And don't think I can't see that you are a *very* bad boy."

The room was small. The walls were lined with book binding equipment and a plethora of paddles, canes and whips. A worktable sat in the center of the room with a few old books on its surface.

"I don't hold with flaunting of the rules or habitual lateness; it's like stealing."

"But it's not stealing, it's more…"

"Take down your pants and place your hands on the edge of the table."

He began to unbuckle his belt and undo his pants. As he slid them down his legs he said, "I didn't mean to steal anything, I couldn't…"

"And the underwear."

"Yes, ma'am." He removed his underwear and his cock sprang up against his belly.

"Yes, now I can see that you are a very, very bad boy who must be taught a lesson."

He felt her hand smooth the skin over first one bared

cheek and then the other as pre-come dripped from his straining cock. There was a brief pause, and then the feeling of wind against his bottom right before a great, hard smack struck his right cheek, soon followed by the same sensation of wind and hard smack on his left cheek. He felt the breath leave his lungs.

"I will give you seven strokes of the paddle for the seven months of late returns." She continued with the harshest paddling he'd ever had until, in the end, he was sobbing. She hung up the paddle and gently caressed his burning rear and, as he leaned down to pull his pants up, he realized that yes, there was a definite odor of sex.

"No more late returns. If the behavior continues, I'll be forced to take more drastic measures." She opened a drawer in the worktable and, among the contents, he spied chains, clamps, weights, butt plugs and electrical devices before she closed it again.

Trying to keep the smile off his face, cock painfully hard, he followed her back to the front office and made for the door. "Ahem," she said, "Aren't you forgetting something? That will be $3.80, please."

He left with a hand on his bottom and one on his cock, dreaming of the many late library books in his future.

About the Authors

Louisa Bacio is the author of six erotic novels, including the paranormal series *The Vampire, The Witch & The Werewolf*, and numerous steamy stories. Her *Sex University* trilogy is available from Riverdale Avenue Books. Drop in for a visit **www.louisabacio.com**.

Trinity Blacio is the #1 Amazon bestselling romance writer of paranormal erotic romance for the series *Running in Fear* and *Masters of the Cats*, as well as a number of dark fantasy, erotic romance, erotic horror and ménage titles. She is a PAN member of the Ohio chapter of Romance Writers of America, and is the bestselling author of a paranormal stepbrother romance series that made her an All Romance eBooks and Siren bestselling author.

Coming from a split family, Trinity Blacio has lived in Minnesota, California, Michigan and Florida, but eventually settled in the state where she was born—Ohio. She has an associate's degree in psychology and social work from Lorain County Community College, and a bachelor's degree in psychology from Cleveland State University.

You will find her on Facebook, Twitter and Goodreads. She loves to talk with all her fans.

Ryan Field is the author of over 100 published modern gay romance novels and stories, including *An Officer and*

His Gentleman, Fangsters Vampire series, *The Rainbow Detective Agency* series, and best-selling *Virgin Billionaire* series. You can check out his web site, www.ryan-field.blogspot.com, and follow him on Facebook, Instagram, and @ryanfield on Twitter.

Award-winning author and editor **DL King** has been writing blistering erotica for more than a decade and is known as a master of femdom, from her ground-breaking Melinoe novels to her anthology of femdom stories, *Under Her Thumb*, from Cleis Press. A collection of her own femdom short stories, *Her Wish is Your Command*, as well as A *Scarlet Christmas,* a female dominant erotic retelling of Dickens' A Christmas Carol have been published by Riverdale Avenue Books.

Oleander Plume lives in Chicago, Illinois, with her husband, two daughters and a pair of obnoxious cats. While she writes in many genres, her favorite is m/m. Or m/m/m. Or m/m/m/m, or … who's counting, anyway?
Horatio Slice: Guitar Slayer of the Universe (published by Go Deeper Press) is Oleander's first full-length novel, but her short stories have appeared in anthologies by Violet Blue, Rachel Kramer Bussel, Shane Allison, Alison Tyler, Neil Plakcy, and F. Leonora Solomon.
Oleander also edited a self-published erotic anthology, titled *Chemical [se]X*, featuring stories centered on the theme of aphrodisiac chocolates.

***USA Today* Bestselling Author Renee Rose** is a naughty wordsmith who writes kinky BDSM and spanking romance novels. Named Eroticon USA's *Next Top Erotic Author* in 2013, she has also won *The Romance Reviews*

Best Historical, Sci-Fi and BDSM awards, *Spanking Romance Reviews*' Best Historical, Erotic, Ageplay and favorite author, and was a finalist for The BDSM Writer's Con Golden Flogger award. She's hit #1 on Amazon in multiple categories in the U.S. and U.K., is often found on the list of Amazon's Top 100 Authors. **Grab six free Renee Rose ebooks, for FREE at Http://owned.gr8.com** *Scoring with Santa*, with co-author Theresa Roemer, and *The Bossman* series are all published by Riverdale Avenue Books.

Jack Stratton is a native Brooklynite, writer, feminist, dandy, switch, and most of all hedonist. He has been writing erotica for ten plus years on his site writingdirty.com and is hard at work on new stories and novels that mix the dirty and the literary.

Lissa Trevor, 2016 IPPY Gold medalist in erotica, is a writer with very few boundaries. She's written a fictional tale of a real gigolo in *The Vegas Virgin*, and helped tell the story of an intersex love affair that turned into an adult movie in *Going for the Gold*. Not a stranger to controversy, her debut novel, *Spank Me, Mr. Darcy*, was a tongue-in-cheek (among other places) version of *Pride & Prejudice*. From *LifeStyle Mirror*: "Fans of classics and historical romances will appreciate this Jane Austen-meets-kink mashup, using *Pride and Prejudice* as the jumping-off point. Do you like bodice-ripping? Oh, there's bodice-ripping, all right, and then some." She steps into the erotic paranormal with her Loose-Id books *Santa Genie* and *Undercover Lover*. And coming in 2018, her erotic multi-paring dystopian novel: *In Too Deep*, will take you to a world where sex is currency. Lissa is a frequent reader at

Riverdale Avenue Book's Between the Covers events. You can find her at http://lissatrevor.weebly.com

Jennifer Williams is an author, editor, cat lady and coffee enthusiast. Her fiction has previously appeared in Women of the Bite: Lesbian Vampire Erotica, and in Vicious Verses and Reanimated Rhymes, a collection of zombie poetry. She has work slated to appear in the upcoming horror anthology Hardened Hearts due out in December 2017 by Unnerving Magazine. When she's not writing she enjoys reading, watching movies, and hanging out with her cat. She also, occasionally, likes to hit things. You can find her on Twitter at @JenWilliams13

About the Editor

Lori Perkins is a published author, book editor and literary agent with three decades experience in publishing newspapers and books. She was the owner and publisher of the Uptown Weekly News in Manhattan's Washington Heights and Inwood in the 80's, as well as an adjunct professor of journalism at NYU. She has written or edited 30 books, 25 of which have been erotic romance anthologies. She was the editor of the very first zombie romance anthology, *Hungry for Your Love,* and the editor of the nonfiction collection of essays *50 Writers on 50 Shades of Grey,* as well as *1984 in the 21st Century* and is the co-author of *Everything You Always Wanted to Know About Watergate (But Were Afraid to Ask).* She is the founder of the L. Perkins Agency, an established New York literary agency with numerous books on the New York Times bestseller list, as well as the Publisher of Riverdale Avenue Books, an award-winning hybrid publisher. She is currently working on a series of naughty historicals with USA Today bestselling author Jamie Schmidt under the nom de plume Lorna James. You can follow her on Twitter at @LoriPerkinsRAB.

If You Liked this Title, You Might Also Enjoy

Holiday Smut: A Collection of Sexy Christmas Stories
Edited by Lori Perkins

Happy MILF Day:
Stories Celebrating Hot Moms
Edited by Lori Perkins

Happy DILF Day:
Stories Celebrating Hot Dads
Edited by Lori Perkins

SuperBowl Smut: A Collection of Erotic Football Stories
Edited by Lori Perkins

Electro-deluxe
By Lori Perkins

Bases Loaded: Baseball Erotica
Edited by F. Leonora Solomon

Tie Me Up: A Binding Collection of Erotic Tales
Edited by F. Leonora Solomon

Amorous Congress: A collection of New Victorian
Erotica
Edited by F. Leonora Solomon